THE WARRIOR
OF WORLD'S END

BOOKS BY LIN CARTER

THE GONDWANE EPIC

The Warrior of World's End
The Enchantress of World's End
The Immortal of World's End
The Pirate of World's End

ZARKON, LORD OF THE UNKNOWN:

The Nemesis of Evil
Invisible Death
The Volcano Ogre
The Earth Shaker

OTHER TITLES:

Beyond the Gates of Dream
The Black Star
The City Outside the World
Kellory the Warlock
The Man Who Loved Mars
The Quest of Kadji
Time War
Tower at the Edge of Time
Tower of the Medusa
The Wizard of Zao

THE WARRIOR OF WORLD'S END

LIN CARTER

WILDSIDE PRESS
BERKELEY HEIGHTS • NEW JERSEY

THE WARRIOR OF WORLD'S END

No portion of this book may be reproduced by any
means, mechanical, electronic, or otherwise, without first
obtaining the permission of the copyright holder.
For more information, contact:

Wildside Press
P.O. Box 45
Gillette, NJ 07933-0045
www.wildsidepress.com

Copyright © 1974 by Lin Carter

Cover art by Vincent Di Fate

FIRST WILDSIDE PRESS EDITION:
JANUARY 2001

CONTENTS

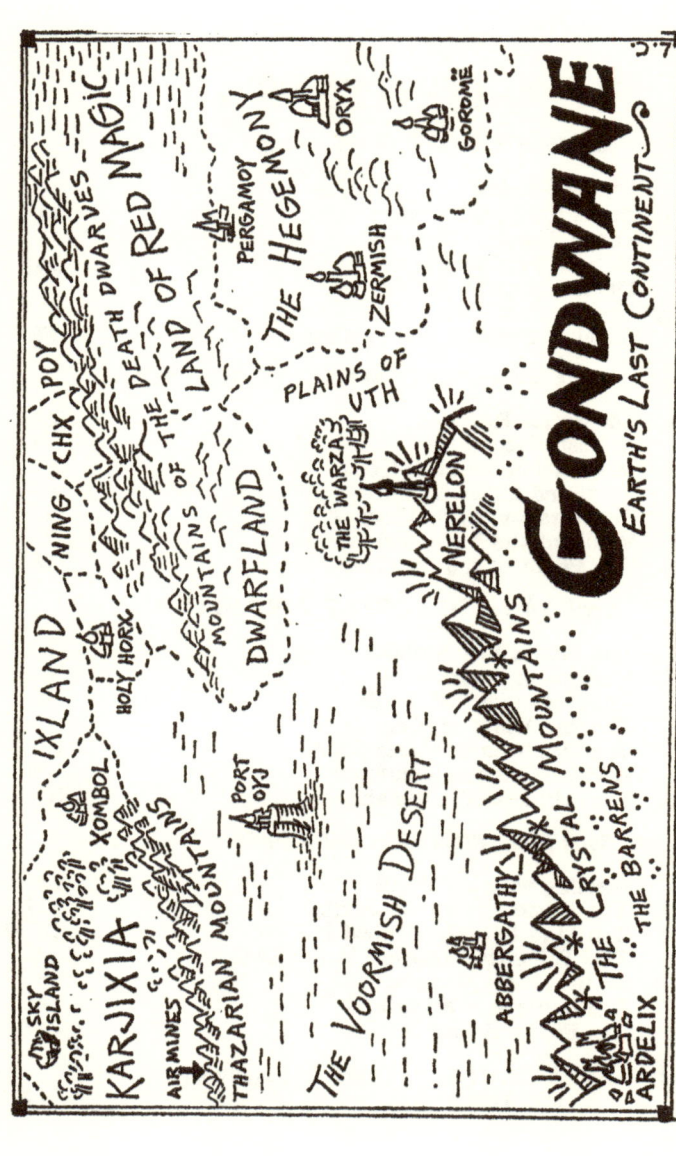

THE WARRIOR OF WORLD'S END

The First Book
of the Gondwane Epic

I see Gondwane as it shall be in the untold ages of dim futurity, near the time when the Earth shall be man's habitation no more, and the great night shall enfold all, and naught but the cold stars shall reign. The first sign of the end ye shall see in the heavens, for Lo! the Moon is falling, falling. And there shall come a man into the lands, a man not like unto other men, but sent from Galendil.

—OTH KANGMIR,
the Book Imperishable

Book One

THE ADVENT OF SILVERMANE

The Scene: **Northern YamaYama-Land: The Barrens; Zermish in the Hegemony; the Plains of Uth.**

The Characters: **A Construct; several Godmakers; a Pseudowoman; haruspices, seers, diviners; an Illusionist; Burgesses, soldiers, citizens; sixty thousand Indigons.**

1.

THE BLUE RAINS

At the western end of the Crystal Mountains there flourished in former ages the city of Ardelix. Once it had been a great center of a race called Hybrids of Phex, but at the end of the period of which I write it had long been abandoned to ruin by the Phexians, who were themselves extinct, having succumbed to the Laughing Plague half an eon earlier.

South of the Ardelix ruins begins a shadowy and dubious borderland known as The Barrens. This desolate region extends the length of the mountain range and is seldom, if ever, visited by True Men. Those infrequent travelers who indeed venture into these parts of Gondwane the Great, Earth's last and mightiest continent, prefer to circumambulate the entire Crystal range, rather than attempt to cross over by any of the passes through the mountains. The reason for this is that the ghosts of the vanished Phexians, trapped forever between the reflecting planes of the glassy peaks and, by now, gone mad from hopelessness, are sometimes glimpsed among the mountains. They extract, it is said, unwholesome tribute from the occasional traveler who is rash and imprudent enough to intrude into the mirrored hell wherein they must wander eternally.

Early in the last century of the Eon of the Falling Moon* an itinerant periaptist and his wife were journeying to the Realm of the Nine Hegemons north of the Crystal Mountains. They were riding along the edges of The Barrens when, driven by a sudden storm to seek refuge among the crystal boulders, they made an unexpected discovery.

---

* The Eon of the Falling Moon ended about 700,000,000 A.D. Tradition asserts that the event whereof I write took place some seventy years before the termination of this eon and the beginning of the next, that of the Silver Phoenix. An approximate date of 699,999,930 A.D. may therefore be assigned to the appearance of Ganelon in the supercontinent Gondwane.

11

During this period of the year the regions of Northern YamaYamaLand are frequently subjected to a mysterious precipitation known as the Blue Rains. No savant has yet explained the origin of these uncanny rainstorms, but they are popularly believed to be poisonous. This may have been sheer superstition, of course, but Phlesco the periaptist was not the sort of man who willingly gambles with death. Hence, when the skies deepened to somber violet and the first azure mists came seething down, the little man thumped his bony heels into the ribs of his birdhorse, cried a peremptory warning to his wife, and turned the beaked head of his mount into The Barrens, where husks of enormous crystals lay strewn about, having been dislodged by lightning bolts from the glittering and glassy scarps which marched along the horizon to the north.

They reached the shelter of one of the nearer crystals without harm, although Phlesco's yellow-striped robe was now spotted with stains of greenish ooze which he hastily scrubbed away, jittering prayers to the seventeen major godlings of his native pantheon that calamity might be averted from him and his.

The wife of the talisman-maker, being a Nonhuman, and thus invulnerable to those poisons which might discomfort a true member of Homo sapiens, ignored the raindrops staining her own garments and stood at the edge of their shelter, watching the storm-swept scene with fascination. The Blue Rain fell in a very fine mist of droplets, like a descending fog, and, as veil on veil of misty blue thickened, the quality of daylight changed to a dim and mysterious azure light. It darkened soon enough, split through by dazzling flares of purple lightning which were reflected in blinding flashes from the faceted and mirrorlike slopes of the mountains. As the blue mist thickened into wetness and mingled with the dull crystal sand of The Barrens, it became pools and puddles ranging in hue from royal purple, deep violet, rose-azure, metallic blue, pure vermilion, and a host of other shades and permutations of colors too rare or too subtle for her to give them a name.

By this time the downfall had become quite heavy. From down-drifting mists, the rain had become a vertical deluge. Crystal powder boiled beneath the impact of a million pelting raindrops; blue rivers sluiced violently between the crystal boulders, dislodging some, which briefly floated like ungainly elfin argosies upon the maelstrom, eventually capsizing.

"Wife, come away before you are splashed," her husband said fretfully from within the hollow shell of crystal. She was about to comply with his command, as was her usual habit, when an astounding sight seized her attention.

The azure deluge had, a split second before, been lit to noonday dazzle by an unearthly flare of purple lightning. By the sudden glare she had seen, or thought she had seen, a naked and gigantic man stumbling through the downpour. A man taller than any True Human she had ever seen, with the broad, powerful shoulders, the swelling thews and narrow waist and lean hips and long, sinewy legs of a gladiator or a hero out of legend. But what man would be here in The Barrens, a region rumored to be unwholesome in the extreme? And why would he be devoid of clothing and of weapons? Perhaps she had merely glimpsed a mirage, born of the blue flood and the sudden flash of astral fire. . . .

She waited for another flare of lightning, and when, in a moment, it came, she saw again the bare and mightily muscled figure, stumbling among the lurching crystals, sliding and floundering in the sparkling blue mud.

"Husband! There is a man out there in the storm!"

"More's the pity for him, then," the periaptist said peevishly. "Let him seek refuge from the storm as we did. *I* am certainly not going to venture out into that hellish flood, and neither are you." Despite the finality in his words, the old artisan crept to the opening and peered out distastefully into the downpour. He, too, saw the naked, stumbling giant, his magnificent physique streaming with the blue precipitate, as nude as a river-nix, stumbling and floundering among the boulders.

"We must help the poor man, husband," his wife said. Phlesco sighed and groaned. But he knew that tone of voice, and was well aware that when Iminix spoke with just that patient, reasoning intonation in her voice, it was best for his peace of mind and for the serenity of his domestic arrangements that he perform the slight task she desired of him.

Among the thirty or forty amulets, periapts, scarabs, and charms he wore about his scrawny neck was a singularly potent talisman of mauve sandstone which bore the sigil of Urgive, a minor godling of the Vemenoid Pantheon worshiped chiefly by desert-dwellers. Urgive reputedly felt a detestation for water so extreme that his protection, if properly evoked, might serve to deflect the azure deluge, at least long enough for Phlesco to haul the naked and floundering giant into the shelter of their crystal husk.

In the end it took both of them to drag the big man in out of the downpour, for he seemed unable to understand what was happening to him or what it was they were trying to do. Thoroughly soaked by the time they had the giant safe within the hollow crystal, Phlesco huddled next to his wife, feebly cursing the desert godling whose protection had, after all, proved insufficient to deflect the downpour.

The Blue Rain, as he soon discovered, worked on human skin like a dye. Phlesco the periaptist was blue from crown to heel for the entire following month, until at last he regained his accustomed sallow umber.

2.

IMINIX THE PSEUDOWOMAN

The Rains ebbed to drizzle, and then to mist again, and by an hour before sunfall they ceased altogether and the two were able to continue their journey.

Of course, there was nothing else to be done but to take the huge youth along with them. Questioning him in an attempt to elicit his name, origin, and circumstances, Phlesco was forced to shrug and give up, for the results were nil. The naked creature, who certainly appeared manlike, did not seem to understand the language spoken by the periaptist. This in itself was odd, for the same universal tongue is spoken across the length and breadth of Gondwane. And, since the land surface of Old-Earth's last continent in this age totaled sixty million square miles—shared between one hundred and thirty-seven thousand kingdoms, empires, city-states, federations, theocracies, tyrannies, conglomerates, unions, principates, and various degenerate, savage, barbarian or Nonhuman, hordes, all holding the same language in common—you could spend a lifetime of journeys without encountering a sentient creature speaking an unfamiliar language.

From this factor, as well as the floundering and ungainly manner in which the young giant handled himself, Phlesco the periaptist sourly surmised the young giant was an idiot, or at least a cretin. But Iminix pointed out, in that patient, reasonable tone, that even if he was mentally defective, that was all the more reason they could not abandon the helpless wretch to die in the wilderness.

And so they took him along to the north country. He did not seem to know how to ride one of the bird-horses, a species of quadrupedal *ornithohippus* which had only evolved into being during the last three-quarters of a million years, so they placed him in the wain with their luggage and few rude pieces of household furniture. Exhausted from his ordeal in the storm, he lapped up the meal Iminix gave him and fell asleep.

Iminix was a mere Pseudowoman from Chuu, and not a True Human at all, but he found her congenial and companionable and—although they could have no children, since she was not actually female in the full sense of the biological term—they got on well enough together. He had purchased her when she was but newly budded from the breeding tree, and the act had been prompted more by pity than desire. The Pseudowomen of Chuu are normally of superhuman beauty and unearthly seductiveness, despite the fact that they are not even mammalian creatures. Iminix had a crooked back and a cast in one eye and would have been destroyed by the Breeding-Master had not Phlesco offered a cube of virgin iridium for her. He was not certain why he had done this, but he himself, as an apprentice Godmaker, had taken the involuntary vows of chastity and thus would have found propinquity to a True Human female a constant annoyance and potentially disruptive to his serenity. Yet he needed a combination cook, laundress, and companion: someone with whom to share his thoughts, his aspirations, and his dreams. So he had purchased Iminix.

As for Iminix, she was at first grateful to Phlesco for having saved her from the shredding machine and the compost pit; later, she came to honestly like the irascible little Godmaker for his real virtues. Despite his generally peevish bossiness, he was a genuinely good man, and when his innate goodness fell short, he could, she found, be persuaded into a needed course of action by an appeal to his vanity. She became very fond of him, and he of her; after they had been together for ninety-three years, he cut away the silver bracelet of ownership which encircled her left wrist and married her according to the rites celebrated in Oth-Yom-Barqa.

Only then did she find that she loved him. Of course, it was forever impossible that she could ever bear him a child. Her own condition precluded any possibility of this, but, then, so did his, for the vows of perpetual chastity made by apprentices to the Godmakers' Guild were irreversible; not by oath alone, but Q-radiation was applied to sterilize the apprentices, and for this no cure had ever been discovered.

Phlesco had graduated with high honors from the college run by the Guild, but Godmakers were something of a glut on the market, he found to his dismay. All the lands about the Smoking Mountains were more than full of them already. So, in the end, he became a traveling periaptist, peddling his wares in town and camp and village, pandering to the superstitions of the seven hundred cults followed by True Humans and Nonhumans in that portion of the supercontinent. It was a bit of a comedown for one trained in the art of designing and creating gods, to be reduced to a humble carver-of-amulets, but it was a living. They made do with what they had, Phlesco and Iminix, and hoped for better times.

After all these years of scrimping and saving, they had finally set aside sufficient funds to journey north to Zermish, where Phlesco determined to open a shop: this was the reason for the journey they were undertaking at the time they found Ganelon.

Of course, they did not know he was Ganelon then.

That first night they camped out under the stars. The Moon had not yet risen—when it did, it would occupy an enormous portion of the sky, and would appear many, many times larger than the Moon known in that remote, forgotten era, the Twentieth Century. The denizens of that lost age would have recognized it, nonetheless, for it was Old Earth's familiar Moon—though it had come far closer to the surface of the planet in the seven hundred million years which had passed since the Twentieth Century.

Some said it had come too close, that soon it would fall and destroy Gondwane. And that would destroy the world itself. For this reason, in after ages, the entire age was named the Eon of the Falling Moon.

It did indeed fall, in a sense, later on. But that's another story. . . .

So they took him with them to the city. I suppose it was Iminix, with her frustrated dreams of maternal instinct, who impelled them to adopt him. She was, at any rate, too tenderhearted to merely abandon the great helpless lout to perish by the side of the road. Phlesco grumbled and argued, but finally gave in.

He was hardly the babe of which poor Iminix had dreamed. He stood three and one-half *farads* in height, which made him taller by head and shoulders and upper chest than an ordinary man* and his physical development was extraordinary. From the smoothness of his skin, the beardlessness of his face, and a certain air of boyish candor and innocence about him, Phlesco assumed him to be a youth, for all of his superlative height and magnificent physique. Some age between fifteen and twenty he surmised.

He would have been mightily disconcerted if he discovered that, in one sense of the word, Ganelon's age was two hundred million years when they found him wandering in The Barrens, and that, in another sense of the word, he had then been barely seven hours alive.

But we shall get to this matter a bit further on.

Despite his huge size and superb development, he was totally lacking in muscular coordination and as witless as a babe. This, I think, is what most strongly appealed to the protective maternal instincts of Iminix. He was nothing more than an overgrown baby. When he attempted to walk he fell down as often as not; when he tried to speak he babbled mindlessly; and when she tried to feed him he drooled the pap down his massively thewed chest.

But in time he learned to eat and drink, and to walk unclumsily. Phlesco glumly resolved he had been less than accurate in his first estimation of Ganelon's intelligence: he was neither an idiot nor a cretin, but merely a moron.

Iminix, however, stubbornly refused to believe this. Ob-

---

* I reckon this measure to be several inches over seven feet in height.

serving the boy's progress in learning to care for himself, she believed him to be of completely normal intelligence. But in her opinion his intellectual capacities were almost completely *potential*, or had been when first they had glimpsed him stumbling about in the Blue Rain. She argued that a newborn babe is as mindless and uncoordinated as a drooling idiot, too, but that he may mature into an intellect of genius; that his capacities, therefore, are completely potential, at birth. So, she suggested, it was with Ganelon.

"Wife, there is no arguing with you!" Phlesco sighed. "But I must say I have yet to hear of a newborn babe who stands seven and a half feet tall, and weighs four hundred and seventy pounds!"*

"Husband, there are very many things you have yet to hear of, I am sure," Iminix replied, in that patient, sweetly reasonable tone of voice, against which Phlesco knew better than to argue. "And I am going to begin teaching Ganelon how to talk and read and write."

Phlesco returned to work on a fetish, deciding the easiest course was to let her have her own way. Things usually worked out best that way.

The azure pigment in the Blue Rains did not adhere to Ganelon's hide as it had to Phlesco's epidermis. His natural coloring was dark bronze, and he was remarkably handsome. His eyes were black and magnetic, under inky, scowling brows—at least when he frowned. But he seldom frowned in those days, for he was very happy. The black eyes and brows formed a rather startling contrast to his hair, for this was a long, flowing mane of incredible sparkling silver. I do not mean to imply by this term that he had the white hair, bleached by extreme age, which is sometimes called "silvery." I mean *silvery*; his mane was composed of innumerable fine strands of supple, metallic silvery hue. This was not a trait of True Men, and so a Nonhuman strain was suspected in his ancestry.

No particular social stigma was attached to such mixed ancestry. In these, commonly believed to be the Last Days, trueborn humanity was a dwindling, perhaps a dying, species. Evolution had continued its subtle, invisible surgery amid the gene pool of Terrene life-forms, and

---

* That's not what Phlesco actually said, of course, but I have resolved to simply translate all such common, everyday terms from this point on, in order to save my footnotes for the conveyance of genuinely important information.

many new races of beasts as well as sentient humanoids
had arisen to challenge Man's dominance of the Last Continent in the Twilight of Time. The Pseudowomen of Chuu
were but the most harmless of these curious and often inimical creatures; the Halfmen of Thaad, the Death
Dwarfs, the mobile and perhaps sentient Green Wraiths,
the Strange Little Men of the Hills, the Tigermen of
Karjixia, the Talking Beasts, the Stone Heads of Soorm,
and many another breed shared the supercontinent with
True Men, and often on an even footing.

No, Iminix knew that Ganelon was not completely human. His skin, for example, was very much tougher than
the delicate tissue of epidermis worn by Homo sapiens; his
skin was supple and flexible, but as tough as seasoned
leather. And his flesh itself was much more dense than
that of humankind, and could sustain without so much as
a bruise a blow that would have pulped the flesh and shat-
tered the bones of an ordinary man. His bones were three
times harder than steel.

He had nine senses, although he did not until much
later discover how to use the four that were extra human.

His vitality and stamina were that of thirty men. He
could run faster than a bird-horse, even one bred for racing, and he could sustain the pace for more than one hundred miles. He could go six months without eating, and
eighty-six days without water.

It was obvious to all that he was a superman, a hero.

But to Iminix he was her babe—no, not quite that: her
son.

3.

HAPPY TIMES
IN ZERMISH

The City to which Phlesco and Iminix the Pseudowoman had been traveling when they discovered Ganelon Silvermane wandering in the wilderness was named
Zermish. It was sometimes called the City of Talismans,

from its principal industry, which was the manufacturing of varieties of amulets.

The city stood to the north of the Crystal Mountains in the Realm of the Nine Hegemons, a loose confederacy of mostly independent city-states each of which was ruled by its own hereditary Hegemon. The entire country was governed lightly by the nine-member Hegemonic Council which convened twice yearly to decide on things like taxes and tariffs and the like. The cities of the Hegemony, counting clockwise from Zermish at the western border, were Pergamoy, Sabdon, (which was the northernmost), Aphelis to the east, Iblix and Goromé to the south; and, in the center of the Hegemony, Oryx, Jargo, and Nambaloth. The capital of the entire confederacy, if it had one, was probably Oryx; it was there, anyway, that the Hegemons met for their biannual councils.

It was generally a peaceful and pleasant country and a good place to live. The peasants were not downtrodden serfs, groaning under the licentious whims of a land-owning aristocracy, because there wasn't any land-owning aristocracy. The Hegemons had passed laws against the existence of dukes, barons, princes, earls, marquises, counts, vaivodes, margraves, beys, and nabobs, figuring one Hegemon per city-state was aristocracy enough.

It was one of the more recently founded nations in this part of central northeastern Gondwane. Its history, dated back only thirty-two thousand years (give or take a couple of centuries), which made it rather youngish as nations went on Old Earth these days.

Zermish itself was a medium-sized city with a red stone wall around it. This wall was pierced by seventeen gates, one for each sign of the zodiac.* The major boulevards were paved with stone and lined with shade trees; fountains splashed and sprayed in twenty-four squares, plazas, forums, and bazaars; the Hegemonic Palace was built in the outmoded Hadhazy style of architecture popular in these parts a hundred thousand years ago—a concentric system of buildings facing inward and connected at three levels by aerial bridges, with the entire structure topped by

---

* The zodiacal signs recognized in this era consisted of seventeen Talking Beasts, mythological creatures, and varieties of Non-humans. In the correct order, these signs were that of the Gryphon, Licorne, Su, Bazonga, Mantichore, Lamussa, Basilisk, Yoop, Catobleps, Mandragon, Gyraphont, Myriapod, Firedrake, Minimal, Wyvern, Merwoman, and Spurge.

a ring of colossal statues, each identical to the tiniest degree, representing the six thousand, nine hundred and thirty-three Hegemons of the Zermetic Dynasty. Each of the Hegemons who ruled Zermish were virtually the same personage, for the sperm plasm of the First Zermetic Hegemon—Argelibichus the Perpetual—was still preserved in an Eternity Tank, and from this original ancestral sampling the wife of each regnant Hegemon in turn was ritually impregnated with a ceremonial catheter of stain-resisting platinum.

For reasons such as the above, the long history of Zermish was a singularly uneventful one.

The shop which Phlesco purchased with his life's savings stood, of course, on the Street of the Godmakers.

The principal industries of Zermish were periaptry, talismaning, and amulet-smithing. The goods thus produced by the craftsmen of these several related Guilds were then exported to the religious, magical, occult, or mystical markets in the neighboring countries, and sometimes were sold as far away as Phoy or Barchemis, or even the Kakkawakka Islands, which were in the Third Lesser Inland Sea, near Chuu.*

Phlesco set himself up as a Godmaker with his certificate of graduation, a handsome parchment of simulated demonskin adorned with gold and purple and scarlet seals, ribbons and sigils, prominently displayed over the main counter. In no time he enjoyed a thriving trade, for his concepts, design innovations, and visual renderings were new and exciting to the Zermishmen, who rarely got a chance to view the latest styles and fashions popular among the Godmakers of the Smoking Mountains.

The scrawny old artisan was delighted by his success. He had hardly dared permit himself the hope of such a welcome, after all those meager years of carving talismans and periapts—a trade to which, had his Godmaking venture eventuated in failure, he could always have returned. But his fellow Guild-members welcomed him with extreme cordiality, and in no time orders and commissions were pouring in. A barbarian chieftain from the Largroolian plains desired a new godling with thirteen heads, each

---

* Chuu, where Iminix originally budded, is in a region called Caostro, the Land of the Dead Cities, on the northern shore of the Zelphodon.

more hideous than the last, and the whole carved from a single block of *ongga* wood twenty feet high; for that order, Phlescó billed the tribe for five hundred ounces of *glelium*. A shaman from the community of hermits who inhabited fumaroles in the peak of Mount Ziphphiz in Garongaland commissioned him to create a god of the winds and the airy spaces which should be as light as air itself, but durable as steel. Phlesco executed the commission by shaping an immense bubble of blown glass filled with helium, the glass impregnated with strands of boron twelve molecules thick and ninety million long, and thus unbreakable. For that, his fee was princely.

The new munificence meant a porcelain oven for the kitchen, woven silk wall hangings, a necklace of crystallized sphinx-eyeballs threaded on catgut, and a court dress composed of eleven thousand multicolored feathers. These, of course, were for Iminix, who might not have been human but was essentially a woman.

Human nature being much the same in every age, it was possible that Phlesco's fellow-craftsmen might have resented his sudden success and come to regard him as a rival and an upstart foreigner. Such, I am happy to state, did not prove to be the case. Each Godmaker had his own speciality, and none had cause to resent the success of another; old Galzolb, for instance, tended to execute colossuses, his principal achievement having been to carve an entire mountain into the form of the Sleeping God of Xoom in his youth; sprightly, affable Izzilp, on the other hand, sculpted gods in miniature, and once reproduced the entire pantheon of the Zul-and-Rashemba mythos on one side of a single seed pearl; and Karmph made gods of adamantine metals perishable only by needles of atomic fire; and Lloim made his of cloth, papier-mâché, feathers, and balsa. To each man his own chosen area of expertise, that was the rule; and the success of any artisan in Zermish benefited all the Zermishmen.

Just beyond the Street of the Godmakers, where it terminated in Qualish Square, a side alley led into the Avenue of Seers. Therein resided the fortune-tellers, astromancers, horoscopists, diviners, haruspices, and all such persons who followed the more mundane of the divinatory arts. The great Street of the Prophets was on the other side of the city; there, of course, lived the major foretellers of the future, who were favored by the Gods. Such at least was their claim.

But in the shabby little Avenue of Seers lived Phlesco's crony, a haruspex named Slunth. His shop was small and disreputable, the windows fogged with dust and garlanded with cobwebs, the gilt charactery all but faded into illegibility on the small sign that hung creaking over his door.

Slunth had studied haruspexy at the Collegium of the Sacred Sciences and Divinatory Arts in Great Veladon on the coasts of the Third Lesser Inland Sea, where the River Zelphus merges its waters with the waters of the cataract known as Thundermountain Falls. He was, thusly, more or less a fellow-countryman of Iminix, and in his way a colleague of Phlesco. A friendship grew up between the God-maker's family and the haruspex.

He enters this narrative only in a minor and unimportant way. That is, it was he who gave Ganelon his name. Until that event Iminix had called the youth by a variety of fond pet-names. Phlesco had referred to him, in his short-tempered way, as Dummy, or Lumpish, or You Simpleton.

When they had been two years in Zermish, Iminix decided it was time the bronze giant had a proper name. Although Phlesco grumbled at the expense, the Psuedowoman took him to the Temple and paid the priest two rods of *qrium* for an auric reading. The results were, said the priest, unintelligible; he did not, however, return the qrium. Then Slunth volunteered to divine the boy's True Name, which was written on the soul, according to the Zul-and-Rashemba mythos, not on the aura as the Oshpazian Mystery believed.

His True Name, he told them, was Ganelon.

But Slunth had seen other things written on Ganelon's soul besides just his name. One of them was so significant, or so astounding, or perhaps both, that he dispatched a message to a magician friend of his, asking him to visit Phlesco's shop when next he was in the city.

This magician was known as the Illusionist of Nerelon; he had formerly lived in Oryx but he no longer resided in that city, having transferred his place of residence to an enchanted palace in the northerly peaks of the Crystal Mountains.

From this fact you might easily have deduced that he was a magician of considerable power and potency, since he obviously had, or believed that he had, little or nothing to fear from the Ghost-Phexians said to haunt those mountains.

The fact of the matter was that he was a. master of Mind Apparitions, and the Ghost-Phexians feared *him*.

What Slunth's note had hinted at concerning the mysterious bronze giant with silver hair, whose antecedents were completely unknown, intrigued the Illusionist. He resolved to pay a visit to Phlesco's shop at the next opportunity.

That afternoon he tried a toss or two of thirty slim ivory rods on a marked table inscribed with symbols of good or ill fortune. It was a minor divinatory art he had learned from Slunth: you could read the broad, general implications of an event or decision from the way the ivory rods fell, forming certain patterns, in certain marked squares.

After studying the way the rods fell, he decided to visit Zermish without delay, and before nightfall he entered the Street of the Godmakers.

4.

PHLESCO THE GODMAKER

The Illusionist found it easy to make friends with Phlesco. The two easiest ways to Phlesco's heart were to praise his work and to pay good money for it.

The Illusionist found no difficulty in praising the craftsmanship of Phlesco, for he had rarely seen better art. Nor did he begrudge Phlesco's prices, for money was nothing to him, and there were a number of small, exquisite eidolons, statuettes, and images he yearned to possess. Phlesco basked in the praise of a knowing connoisseur, and was impressed to be patronized by the Illusionist. The reason for this was that the Illusionist was so superlative in his own area of work that he needed no other name than that of his craft; and from the fact that his features were perpetually concealed behind a mask of lavender vapor it was logical to assume that he had many jealous and vindictive rivals, which only served to enhance one's impression of his standing in his field.

Soon the Illusionist took to dropping into Phlesco's shop quite often. He made no pretense of indifference to Ganelon; indeed, he professed his interest in the bronze giant very early in his relationship with the Godmaker, and with praiseworthy candor admitted it was Slunth who had suggested he visit the shop in order to examine the mysterious youth.

"You truly know nothing of his antecedents, then?" he asked Phlesco.

"Nothing much; he's a good boy, I suppose. Helps around the shop, you know. Handy to have him here when there are heavy idols to lift or blocks of stone to move into the workroom. Not as dumb as I first thought; why, the wife has actually taught him how to speak and to conn his letters."

"You have never deduced anything from the fact that you first discovered him wandering in The Barrens, south of the Ardelix ruins, I take it?"

Phlesco shrugged. Discussions of Ganelon tended to bore him, because he disliked taking the great clumsy oaf seriously.

"May I ask him a few questions?"

"Suit yourself."

The Illusionist turned to Ganelon, who stood behind his adoptive father, ready to serve more of the sparkling green wine when requested to do so. From the incurious expression on his features one would not have known he was aware it was himself they had been discussing.

"Ganelon, my boy, have you ever heard of the Time Gods?"

The young giant shook his head.

The Illusionist then asked him if the words "Construct" or "Time Vault" or "Epiphany" meant anything to him.

He indicated that they did not. The Illusionist soon left; returning to his palace of enchantments, he again consulted a certain huge book attributed to Yathab Shanderzoth the Unknown Prophet. The tome was written in a mode of charactery long obsolete in these parts of Northern YamaYamaLand, and employed a system of abbreviations peculiarly difficult to puzzle out. The volume was known to magicians and sorcerors and wizards of every kind as *Oth Kangmir*, the Book Imperishable.

He read far into the night; and even after turning from the ancient volume his mind was racing so that he could not compose himself for slumber.

Phlesco purported to view his adopted son with sour, peevish dislike. This was not, of course, true. Both members of the childless couple had taken the innocent young giant to their hearts, but Phlesco was uncomfortable in expressions of emotion and spoke harshly to the youth, although he treated him kindly and never punished him when he broke something or forgot an errand.

In his heart, the Godmaker knew that his son was no ordinary being, but an unusual creature destined for incredible deeds. He dreaded the day to come when fate should call Ganelon from the familial hearth to undertake the high and mighty enterprises for which he had been marked from birth.

Once Iminix had demonstrated that Ganelon was able to speak and to understand speech, and as soon as he began to read and write, the Godmaker undertook to give his son the rudiments of an education. The youth showed utterly no facility for learning his father's craft. He was too huge, too clumsy, to master the fine points of Godmaking, and his great hands were obviously shaped to wield the broadsword or the ax or the war hammer rather than the fine chisels and graving tools of periaptist or Godmaker. Phlesco despaired of the boy's future: how could the great, lumbering lout ever master a craft? Was he destined for no better life than to serve as a soldier in the Hegemon's guard, or as a gladiator in the arena? His strength and size seemed aptly fitted for apprenticeship to a blacksmith, but the profession was a lowly one and never, Phlesco vowed, should it be said that the son of a Godmaker spent his days beating out plowshares on a smelly great forge!

The Illusionist of Nerelon seemed extraordinarily interested in Ganelon for some reason. But as yet he had taken no hand in the boy's education; neither had he volunteered any suggestion as to his failure; and he had certainly evinced no interest in taking the giant on as his apprentice.

Time passed. There came wars, or rumors of war, out of the west. The Indigons, it was rumored, were migrating in enormous herds. They were quasihumans, the Indigons, and very dangerous. Generally, they lived as placid ruminants, but when the migrant urge was upon them, they tended to stream down out of the northwest in ever-growing numbers, destroying every human habitation in their path and wreaking frightful havoc.

Never before had they come so close to the cities of the Nine Hegemons. They were said to be in Phynx; they had been seen on the outskirts of Yombok; farmsteads in Quay had been reduced to rubble and Indigon carcasses were found amid the wreckage; they overran the flax plantations on the borders of Ixland; the Hierophant of Holy Horx had hurled interdict and anathema against them, but to little avail. They were moving south toward the Crystal Mountains; they were descending through the country of the Death Dwarfs; they were skirting the borders of the Land of Red Magic. Unless they were somehow stopped, or turned back of their own inscrutable will, they would come up against the Crystal range. Then they could move in only two directions: westerly, toward Abbergathy, or easterly, toward the Hegemony.

It was said the Hegemonic Council would be convened earlier that year than was usual in order to debate the options of dealing with the possibilities of an Indigon invasion. It was said that the Hegemon of Zermish would enlist all able-bodied citizens into a standing militia, since Zermish was the westernmost city of the nine, and the one most likely to be attacked by the Indigons, should they in fact turn east in their migration, instead of west.

Phlesco, now one of the Burgesses of the city, a member of the House of Forty, elected to represent the Guild in municipal matters, argued caution and prudence. Never in recent millennia had the herds come this far; always they had turned back at the barrier of the Crystal Mountains, or westward, to ravage the citadels of Abbergathy and Horroy and Entherdy. There was yet no reason to anticipate that Zermish was in any particular danger. To raise, train, equip, and arm a militia would dig deeply into the city treasury; funds set aside for worthwhile works of civic improvement would be expended to stave off a danger perhaps imaginary. His prudent arguments carried the vote and he went home tired but triumphant.

The Illusionist was sitting in the rear of the shop, drinking Iminix's fayowaddy tea and chatting with Ganelon. His

blur-misted features were, as ever, impenetrable, his tones
suave and casual.

"Greetings, worthy Phlesco! I trust the arguments of
caution and exemplary prudence swayed the Burgesses
from immodest and reckless expenditures?"

"Such, indeed, was the case." The Godmaker grinned,
seating himself before the fire with a weary sigh and ac-
cepting a cup of tea from Ganelon. He stretched his bony
shanks out before the crackling hearth. "What brings you
to our fair city, Magister?"

"I have decided to leave my palace for a time, lest the
migrants become troublous."

"Surely an uncouth handful of wandering Indigons pose
no threat to the safety of Nerelon," Phlesco said, referring
to the Illusionist's enchanted palace.

"The herd is somewhat inadequately termed 'a handful,'
friend Phlesco. There were thirty thousand of the brutes
when they came down past the Land of Red Magic; three
more contingents have swelled their ranks since then, each
numbering ten thousand more."

"You mean there are now . . . hm . . . sixty thousand
Indigons in the herd?" asked the Godmaker, a trifle anxiously. "My goodness! Still, they may turn back—or west,
toward Abbergathy. . . ."

"I think not," murmured the Illusionist. "Another con-
tingent of the herd is even now ravaging Abbergathy,
heading east to join the combined herds north of the Crystal Mountains. They will come east into the Hegemony."

"Great Galendil! What shall we do?"

"You will fight; there is nothing else to do."

5.

THE INDIGONS
TURN EAST

The Illusionist did not plan to outwait the Indigon incursion by staying here in Zermish; that would be foolish, since it was Zermish the Indigons would attack first. He left that evening for Oryx, in the center of the Hegemony.

The news that Abbergathy had already been reduced to flinders caused no rejoicing in Zermetic hearts. Phlesco's faction lost prestige; that of Urukush, a burly-chested, black-bearded theomancer, gained. The Hegemons met hastily, deciding on a stance of warlike preparedness. Each of the nine cities of the Hegemony were to raise and train a militia as soon as possible. Ten thousand pikes, bows, yarmaks, sting-swords, dart-throwers, axes, war hammers, volusks, and pornoi were contributed to the defense of Zermish, since it was deemed most likely that that city stood directly in the path of the herd and would be the first to be under attack.

Ganelon was conscripted into the militia, which was only natural, considering his height and heft.

"What a warrior that nitling would make, had he half a brain!" Urukush lustily boomed. Urukush had been named Warchieftain of the militia by the Hegemon of Zermish. The ruler of the city, Argelibichus the Six Thousand, Nine Hundred and Thirty-Third, was not in the slightest degree warlike; in fact, he was, considering the present dangers in which the realm stood, thought excessively peace-loving. But the bull-necked, sturdy theomancer took to the life of camp and field as one to the war-craft born. He affected a bronze cuirass, molded to suggest bulging and enormous muscles, and a helmet crowned with the branching antlers of the deadly Youk. He was constantly to be seen striding about, bawling lustily, cursing by half the gods in the pantheon. The citizens were willing to take him at face value, and only hoped he would prove to be half as warlike in the field as he seemed to be in the camp. Half should be enough to turn the Indigons into a rout, they joked among themselves.

Sentinels had been dispatched to man outposts high in the foothills and the heights of the Warza, a forest which stood directly in the path of the advancing herds. It had been planned they would pass their signals along by means of flashing mirrors by day, and code fires by night. The city waited to hear what the Indigons would do when they reached the impassable barrier of the mountain range.

The signals came through sporadically.

SIXTY THOUSAND IN SEETHING TURMOIL AGAINST MOUNTAIN WALL, ran the first signal. It had been arranged by order of the Warchieftain that as soon as a signal had been received and decoded, it would be posted on enormous signboards erected above the principal forums and bazaars, spelled out in huge wooden letters laid out in rows.

AN ESTIMATED SEVEN THOUSAND ATTEMPT THE JHELM PASS BUT ARE DRIVEN BACK BY GHOST-PHEXIANS, ran the second signal. Loud cheers broke out among the throng gathered to read the news.

"Perhaps the Ghost-Phexians will drive the entire herd into retreat," one stout Burgess puffed, fingering his medallion importantly. It denoted him as a member of the House of Forty, and therefore a man of affairs and importance.

"Perhaps," yawned a scruffy beggar huddled against the wall of the bazaar. "And perhaps it will goad them into turning east, eh, squire?"

"Nonsense, my man; the House considers the eventuality hardly likely. Only the other day my dear friend, Urukush, was saying to me . . ."

"Who's that again, squire?"

"Urukush, fellow; surely you've heard of our brave and ferocious Warchieftain!"

"Oh, him. Aye, I've heard he's brave with the wenches and ferocious at the dining table. Anything else we have yet to be seen proved."

"Really!" the Burgess snorted, turning away to seek more congenial surroundings. "Impossible fellow!"

"There's another signal going up now, guttersnipe," one of the Burgess' sycophants pointed out. "Now perhaps you'll see the wisdom of the House in action, and the prowess of Urukush evinced."

The beggar grinned at him, displaying an array of slimed and rotting teeth.

"Aye, and perhaps we'll soon see ass-kissers like you squealing under the flaying knives of the Indigons, my pretty lad, if this Urukush of yours isn't quite as bold a fighter as you think him to be."

The languid young man tried a lofty sneer, which didn't quite come off, and hastened to rejoin the retinue which hovered about his lordly patron.

Thus it was that he missed the reading of the sign. A gasp went up as he was squirming his way through the packed crowd. He turned, craning his neck, to read the dreadful message.

THE INDIGONS ARE TURNING EAST AND MARCHING FOR THE WARZA.

Only the squatting beggar found any amusement in the terrible message; but, as his conditions could hardly be any worse, it was his opinion that the conquest of the city and the collapse of the ruling classes could do him little hurt; besides, many the former beggar has become a man of wealth and substance by looting the palaces abandoned by the flight of princes from war-doomed cities.

All that long day the news continued to arrive at sporadic intervals, and each message was less welcome than the last.

The Indigons did not turn aside at the edges of the woodland, but streamed into the forest in their tens of thousands. One by one the sentinels posted atop the giant ongga trees fell silent, brought down by Indigon arrows.

Urukush dispatched outriders, mounted on the fastest bird-horses the city contained, to fire the nearest edge of the Warza. The bird-horses were former racing stallions, highly prized specimens, kept in the stables adjoining the Amphitheater. The outriders whirled away in a cloud of dust.

An hour later a signal came from a lone sentinel in the foothills.

FOREST FIRE EXTINGUISHED BY INDIGONS, AND RIDERS AMBUSHED AT ZAIM ROCK AND SLAUGHTERED TO A MAN.

Twilight came. The first stars ventured forth on the fields of evening. The Temple of Great Galendil opened earlier than usual for a mass prayer vigil. The most highly esteemed diviners, seers, fortune-tellers, and prophets were polled by order of the Hegemon to ascertain the fate of the city. Without exception, their replies were ambiguous.

The militia was served a hot meal and ordered to rest. The guard posts on the walls of the city which looked in the direction of the Warza were trebled, and all the city's gates were closed and locked and barred.

No further signals were received. it was difficult to interpret this. It could be read as a heartening sign that the Indigons were doing nothing in particular, just moiling about. Or it could be taken as bad news; that is, that the last sentinels had been discovered and slain, and that the Indigons were marching upon the city under cover of night.

By moonrise, no further word had come.

By midnight there was still no updating of the last information received.

Shortly after midnight, Hegemon Argelibichus retired to rest in the Pavilion of the Nine Hundred Concubines.

By three o'clock in the morning, Urukush the War-chieftain, having taken aboard too many stirrup cups, stretched out in his tent in full war harness, wrapped himself in a tigerskin coverlet, and went to sleep.

By dawn it was discovered that sixty thousand Indigons were camped before the gates of Zermish.

6.

THE PLAINS OF UTH

Wrapped in his tigerskins against the morning chill and damp, Urukush viewed the Indigon herd with growing consternation. He had not realized they were quite so fearsome of aspect, nor quite so manlike in their intelligence. While they were only four feet tall, on the average, they were also four feet broad, with arms and shoulders that would have made a gorilla look puny. They wore plates of steel and scraps of dragon-leather, and, as nature had already outfitted their heads with blunt, sharp-pointed horns, no helmets.

For weapons they clenched branches of trees in their enormous, four-fingered paws. Some of them held iron bars thirteen feet long; others held hammers three times the weight of a True Man. They waddled back and forth before the walls, waving these frightful weapons and bellowing like gigantic bullfrogs. Their eyeballs were the size of human fists, and shone the color of fresh blood. They had no noses, no genital organs, and their hide was colored deep blue, and was reputedly as tough as oakwood. They each weighed about a quarter of a ton.

They were completely terrifying. Suddenly, Urukush wondered why in the name of the Thirty Gods he had ever sought the office of Warchieftain in the first place. Well, there was no use crying over spilled blood, until it was actually spilled. The job was his and there was nothing else to do but to get on with the day's sanguinary business.

Morning progressed. The Hegemon, who had been expected to make an appearance at the head of his troops when they marched to battle with the Indigons, failed to show up. The palace issued a statement to the effect that the Gods had seen fit to visit him with a sick headache. Nonetheless, he conveyed his heartiest wishes for a successful battle to Urukush and his subchieftains, and promised them state funerals.

Glumly, the black-bearded general prepared for the inevitable. Citizens had been gathering for the past hour and a half on rooftops and balconies facing the besiegers, in order to command the best possible views of the conflict. Enterprising vendors were already hawking fruitcakes, fresh vemble berries, and mulled spice wine to the expectant audience.

The militia marched from the three gates which fronted on the Indigon herd, advancing in columns of ten abreast. Booming and gobbling in a threatening manner, the Indigons gave ground until the front ranks had reached the center of the Plains of Uth, which stretched from the west wall of the city all the way to the edge of the Warza. They then attacked the three columns from all sides simultaneously. Urukush, who had taken up a strategic position in the rear, so as to be able to collate battle reports more efficiently, could see nothing of the conflict, which was veiled in clouds of dust. All he could hear were the sounds of battle: the bullfrog booming of the blue dwarfs, the screech of bird-horses, the hoarse screams and shouted war-cries of the Zermishmen, the clank and clang of edged weapons striking cuirass, shield, and helm.

In a few moments, however, the warriors of Zermish emerged from the dust-cloud, running in all directions, pitching away their swords and pikes and yarmaks in order to lighten themselves for some serious running. Urukush signaled the reserve battalions into action; these were foot soldiers armed with vorple blades steeped in venomberry juice, and pornoi, which were razor-thin, jag-edged metal throwing discs, hurled by slings. He also deployed a troop of mounted archers who carried dart-hurlers. Then he prudently withdrew to the rearmost rank in order to marshal his remaining forces for an all-out assault, making certain that his command post was stationed within easy running distance of the Catobleps Gate, which stood open.

The Indigons made short work of the reserves and came waddling to meet the mounted warriors, uttering deep-chested cries. The bird-horses sensibly bolted before the advance of the waddling blue horrors, pitching the hapless archers out of their saddles. The few archers who managed to get their dart-hurlers into action cut bloody swaths through the mob of growling, gobbling Indigons before being crushed by them. Urukush decided to take up a new station atop the barbican tower of the gate, so as to have an unimpeded view of the carnage his doughty warriors were inflicting on the herds. Before he was able to slip away, however, a sharp-eyed adjutant called his attention to a remarkable event taking place far behind the front line of the Indigon advance.

The spearhead of one of the long-broken troop columns had stood and fought, for some reason which seemed unaccountable. Now that the rest of the column had fled and the dust of battle cleared, it could be seen that the Zermishmen had formed a large fighting square, locking their kite-shields together, and were still holding firm, slugging it out with the Indigons.

"Looks like that huge boy of Phlesco the Godmaker is leading them," the adjutant said, shading his eyes against the sunglare.

"Admirable; the old Zermish spirit," Urukush said nervously. "I shall see he is mentioned in dispatches. Now I believe I will move the command post to the barbican tower to have a better view. . . ."

"Great Galendil, look at that boy fight!" the adjutant marveled, voicing a low whistle. "He has reformed the square into arrowhead formation, and they are cutting into the main body of the Indigons, with him in the point position. I knew he was big and strong, but I didn't realize he was *that* strong! Why, he's picking up the Indigons and throwing them at each other, as a child hurls pebbles at bottles!"

"Fine work; trained him well; 'Hero of Uth' I shall call him in the obituaries. Now, Xergal, we must be going. There are several parties of Indigons heading this way. . . ."

"Gods and Demigods, the Indigons are backing away from his advance! They are fleeing and the men behind him are charging the line! The boy—Ganelon, that's his name—is a bowshot ahead of them, his strange silvery long hair flashing like a bright war banner through the murk! They follow him as one follows a holy standard! Saints and Sages, three parties of dismounted archers have cut their way to join the isolated troop, and are making a gallant stand. Now some of the Indigons are turning back from chasing our fleeing troops, in order to squelch this thorn in their rump, as you might call it. Urukush, we must send reinforcements to help them."

"*What* reinforcements? Except for my private guardsmen, everybody else has run away!"

"Then we must take the guards and ride to their side ourselves; the Indigons are not invincible after all. They seem to fear the huge boy as if he were some supernatural personage. Avatars and Demiurges, he just brained one with a single blow of his fist! He fights like a superman; he bears a charmed life, I swear!"

"Xergal, I have decided to put you in command of my guards," said Urukush. "Do what you can to rescue the gallant hero of the Battle of Uth."

"But where will you be?" inquired the adjutant.

"I must have an urgent consultation with the Hegemon as to our defensive tactics, once we are completely withdrawn from the field and the Indigons mount against us. Go with Galendil, and see if you can't bring back the body of what's-his-name for interment among the Sacred

Heroes of Zermetic Memory," said Urukush, backing hastily away in the direction of the gate.

Once within the city wall, the Warchieftain adjusted his expression to one of tight-lipped stern grimness, and rode for the Hegemonic Palace in his most straight-backed and martial manner. Argelibichus had taken to his couch, the royal physicians informed him, but they would convey to the monarch the results of the Warchieftain's briefing at a later time. Urukush painted a lurid word-picture of the conflict which few veterans of the battle would have recognized, refreshed himself with a stoup or two of wine and a nibble of pastry, and rode back to the Catobleps Gate to observe in dignified and stoic silence the defeat of his outnumbered but doggedly resisting heroes.

Instead he looked upon a scene of astonishing reversal of fortune. The troops who had gathered about the Godmaker's mentally retarded but outsized foundling had now trebled in number. Obviously, some of the troops which had fled earlier had taken heart from Ganelon's stand, and had gone out to join him and his fellows. The Zermish outpost, now totaling nearly two thousand men, were in rectangle formation by this time, lodged securely behind a breast-high wall composed entirely of Indigon carcasses. From behind these gory fortifications they flung a storm of darts and pornoi into the wavering lines of Indigons, who seemed reluctant to charge the rectangle. Ganelon could clearly be seen, standing atop the wall of corpses, hurling bronze spears and boulders, plucked from the earth of the rock-strewn plain. His bright mane flashed through the murk like a beacon.

Emerging from the several directions in which they had fled, quantities of crestfallen Zermish troops were now gathering into small, disorganized bands, which began cutting their way into the central portions of the plains where the ringed battalions held firm. The mob of Indigons withdrew from their advance as if reluctant to face them. Much of the war spirit had gone out of the waddling blue monsters; their huge scarlet eyeballs rolled in dread toward the gigantic and heroic figure of Ganelon. They fumbled at their weapons, mumbling among themselves; some of them at the edges of the herd had begun breaking away from the main body and were ambling off to the north, toward the Land of Red Magic.

Urukush could scarcely credit the evidence of his own

senses. But there was no doubt about it: although the Zermishmen had suffered very considerable losses, the brave stand óf Ganelon and the warriors who had stood beside him had broken the spirit of the Indigons; once demoralized, it seemed the rudimentary intelligence of the blue monsters was insufficient to maintain the belligerent posture. Soon they were straggling northward in thousands, then tens of thousands.

By nightfall, Ganelon and his weary, victorious, dusty and disheveled troops reentered the city by the Mandragon Gate and moved to the temporary barracks of the militia through wildly cheering throngs of ecstatic citizenry.

The mightiest battle in Zermetic history had ended. And Ganelon had found his true vocation at last.

7.

GANELON RECEIVES HIS AGNOMEN

The following day, Argelibichus, making a speedy recovery from the sick headache which had unfortunately prevented him from leading the militia into battle, reviewed the Heroes of Uth in the great Ruxomian Square before the Hegemonic Palace. Urukush had initially intended to lead his brave and valiant warriors in parade before their monarch, but the men who had taken a stand beside Ganelon laughed and hooted when he appeared in his glittering cuirass, and more than a few voices from the ranks suggested he at least give the breastplate a scratch or two, in order to suggest he had been within a thousand yards of the fighting.

In fact, more than one voice volunteered to give the armor its scratches, and himself a few bumps and bruises, if he would care to venture within arm's reach. Seeing the tenor of the militia tended toward surliness, Urukush cautiously stepped aside in favor of Xergal and retired to his quarters on the pretext of a nagging toothache. Xergal, who carried one arm in a sling, broken by an Indigon buffet, and a gash over one eye from an Indigon swipe, was more acceptable to the warriors. But they would have preferred to have been led by the Godsmith's son.

The Hegemon, having already been apprised of the less-than-soldierly behavior of his erstwhile Warchieftain, was unsurprised at the absence of Urukush. Xergal paraded his limping men about the square, or those who were able to walk, at any rate, and accepted the plaudits of the throng with embarrassed nods and stiff little smiles. Those who were too severely injured to march in the triumph were borne on stretchers. Since virtually all of the militiamen had, sooner or later, returned to the Plains of Uth to fight the Indigons (except for a certain number who had not yet turned up, and may still have been running), only Urukush was absent in disgrace.

Ganelon received the loudest and most prolonged ovations. The grinning giant waved cheerfully at the crowd, which pelted him with bouquets, bits of jewelry, nosegays, and, from many of the women and a certain number of men given to peculiar liaisons, small perfumed notes suggesting times and places of assignation. Phlesco, in a place of honor in the reviewing stand reserved for members of the House, swelled visibly with pride. Iminix, seated beside him in her most expensive gown and wearing all the jewelry she possessed, beamed upon her son with true motherly emotion.

Ganelon's prominent role in the stand against the Indigon herd, and his crucial part in driving them into their stampede into the north, had not gone without notice by the many hundreds of citizens who had gathered on rooftop or balcony to watch the battle. He was the hero of the hour, which was no less than the somewhat battered young giant deserved.

Following the parade, the Hegemon made an appearance among his chief wives, councillors, favorites, and those of the concubines he preferred at the moment. He then delivered a victory oration which lasted about two and a half hours and which was hard to hear since his voice was weak and quavery. The interminable speech had been composed during the sleepless hours of the night by his councillors, and like all such productions composed by committees, it was rambling and touched on every subject under the sun, lacking any central theme and straying into virtual incoherence at times. Each of the Hegemon's one hundred and twenty-six councillors, in order to satisfy his own self-importance, had insisted upon adding his own contribution to the document, and the variety of religious sentiments, patriotic themes, suggested public works, civic programs, municipal reorganizations, national enterprises, and legislative innovations which each were mentioned swelled the speech almost beyond the Hegemon's vocal capacities or the patience of his audience. Every councillor had desired to include a reference to one of his own pet projects or favored ideas.

At the end of the speech (which was greeted by a prolonged burst of applause simply because it had had an ending after all), came an extraordinarily rare ceremonial called the Bestowal of the Zermetic Agnomen.

The Agnomen was the highest honor a Hegemon could give, and the rarest privilege a citizen of the Hegemony could earn. Only eight individuals in the entire history of Zermish had received the Agnomen, and since the city was at this time slightly more than thirty-two thousand years old, it can easily be deduced that the Agnomenial requirements were extraordinarily stringent.

The Bestowal was made, of course, on Ganelon. And, in comparison with the boring and interminably rambling victory speech, it was terse and to the point. This was due to the fact that the text of the Bestowal was fixed by tradition, hallowed by custom, and sanctified by glorious history.

" ... And henceforth to time's end thou shalt be known as Silvermane of Zermish. No more art thou Ganelon Phlescosson, but Ganelon Silvermane from this moment into the future. We salute thee, Ganelon Silvermane, ninth of our race to be thus honored; bear thou thine Agnomen proudly with thee to a hero's grave with honor untarnished and escutcheon pure of stain; enshrined in the Pantheon of Patriots shalt thine likeness forever be, as thy memory is enshrined forever in the hearts and memories of thy fellow-countrymen!"

The Hegemon then led his people in three rousing cheers to the Agnomenic hero.

And he was Ganelon Silvermane from that time on.

Life soon returned to normal in Zermish once the dead were buried and the victors rewarded. Fast-riding scouts reported the Indigon herds had strayed still further north into the Mountains of the Death Dwarfs, after suffering heavy losses to the scythe-armed automatons the Queen of Red Magic employed in lieu of soldiers. Doubtless the last dwindling remnants of the migrant herds would perish in the narrow passes of Dwarf-land. The safety of Zermish was secured.

As the adoptive father of a national hero, it was only fitting and proper that Phlesco was raised at the next election to the Chairmanship of the House. As a special mark of favor he was also made, by unanimous assent, a Burgess for life. The Godmaker basked in the esteem of his compatriots; he thought of taking up politics as a career, turning from his craft to the higher art of statesmanship. Iminix, however, eventually dissuaded him from this course of action, pointing out in her patient reasoning way that votes, proclamations, and decrees were not negotiable at the butcher shop or grocer's stall.

Now that the danger had passed by, the Illusionist returned from his stay in Oryx to take up his residence in Nerelon again. He dropped by the Godmaker's shop to congratulate the proud parents of the hero.

"Praiseworthy, indeed, but nothing more than I had expected of Ganelon," he remarked

"Oh?" Phlesco was a bit surprised; he had formerly considered his son an overgrown, lumbering simpleton and had never guessed him capable of such fortitude in the face of the enemy.

"Of course; he is a Construct, and even the Indigons are wary of such. Doubtless they could detect by their sensitive phloigms the vivid aura of superhuman vitality he projects," the Illusionist said casually. He referred to the organ sensitive to the presence of supernatural beings such as demigods, Immortals, apparitions, demons, angelic powers, Gyraphonts, avatars and Divine Heroes.*

---

* This organ is thought to have atrophied to a mere vestigial appendage in True Men as long ago as the Eon of the Thought Magicians, two hundred million years before Ganelon's time.

"A 'Construct,' you say? I remember you have mentioned that peculiar term before in conversation. Exactly what does it mean?"

"I would rather not discuss the matter unless events should prove it necessary, for reasons of my own. Indulge me in this, my worthy Phlesco," the Illusionist replied, somewhat evasively.

"As you wish, of course," said the Godmaker amiably. "But am I to gather that you have some information on the boy's true identity or origins?"

The Illusionist sighed. "I suppose you must; a pity I let it slip. This delicious beverage has the unfortunate facility of loosening the tongue at times."

"Then you know the boy's secret?" persisted Phlesco.

"I believe so, or part of it, at any rate. I suspected it almost from the first. My own poor phloigms, although nowhere near as healthy and well-developed as the organs of the Indigons, are not completely insensitive to the Akashic radiations; were it otherwise I might have become a poet or a scholar, instead of a magician. But I will speak of this matter another time, if conditions decree it so. Restrain your curiosity; there is nothing shameful, malign, or unsettling about Ganelon's true nature, I assure you."

And more than this the Illusionist would not say.

Book Two

SILVERMANE AT NERELON

The Scene: **The Crystal Mountains; the Palace of the Illusionist; the Yembar Chasm; Mount Droom; the Voormish Desert.**

New Characters: **Gyraphonts and Automatons; several Talking Beasts; the Wraith of Vloob Atz; some Ghost-Phexians; the Bazonga.**

8.

THE SECRET REVEALED

The nine members of the Hegemonic Council, desiring to pay homage to Silvermane for his prowess in war and devotion to his city, had a magnificent broadsword designed for one of his towering size. It was all of six feet long, fashioned from sparkling silver wrought to a hardness exceeding that of steel, with a cabochon ruby the size of a boy's fist set in the pommel. Ganelon accepted it gratefully.

Exciting news traveled out of the north. The Queen of Red Magic, who seldom strayed beyond her own borders, would soon pay a state visit to congratulate the Hegemon on his victory, and to discuss trade agreements on mutually acceptable terms between their two realms.

In time she arrived, a stunning figure in scarlet, at once voluptuous and virginal. She arrived in a chariot drawn by matched wyverns whose metallic green plumage formed a striking contrast to her own scarletness. All who saw her could not help but admire her beauty, although it was a trifle unusual to see a being entirely colored red: she had red hair, skin, eyes, and even teeth.

Her entourage included an honor guard of seventy of her famous brass automatons whose rigid metal arms terminated in scythes, axblades, power drills, or immense, wicked-looking hooks. It was at the hands, so to speak, of these metal men that the herds of the Indigons had been thinned before they reached their total destruction in the Mountains of the Death Dwarfs.

At the very mention of the Indigons the Queen, Zelmarine, was observed to shudder fastidiously. She loathed the bluish coloring of the Indigons; it did so clash with her hair.

On the heels of the Red Queen the Illusionist arrived on

a flying visit. He descended in the small yard behind Phlesco's shop and came straight to the point.

"The time has come for me to tell you all that I have learned about Ganelon," he said. "He is, as I have said before, a Construct. That is, an artificial human being genetically tailored for certain talents, abilities, and features. He was created in the tissue vats of the Time Gods, a weird race who formerly dwelt in the west and who possessed an uncanny ability to foresee coming events. They were destroyed two hundred million years ago in the great meteor rains of the Eon of the Thought Magicians; yet before their extermination, which they of course foresaw, they planned ways in which to help humanity to avert, circumvent, or nullify major perils and calamities."

"But how could they—" Phlesco began, helplessly.

"Let me finish—time is growing short. According to tradition, these superheroes, the product of advanced biological engineering, were buried in Time Vaults concealed in geologically secure locations about Gondwane, each timed to open when the hour of danger was nigh. Some savants believe the Time Vaults purely mythical, for only one is known to have opened within recent history, that which contained the Thinker of Aopharz, that astonishing and prodigious personage deemed responsible for the continued survival of the Thirtieth Empire of Grand Velademar, else doomed to extinction beneath the grinding hooves of the Urghazkoy Horde. No other such Vault is known to have actually opened."

"But I don't understand why you—"

"I have exactly thirty-seven minutes in which to save your son from a peculiar and atrocious doom; so if you will *please* permit me to conclude without these interruptions! The so-called Time Gods are, however, considered to have inserted into the race by genetic timing any number of superior individuals who rose to prominence in subsequent ages. Such as the Ninth Magistrate of Trantain, the famous Pluralist of Mandragon, and Phosphotex Calgalgandar, to name only three. It was the Magistrate, you will recall who solved the Safetilian Dilemma, while the Pluralist succeeded in eliminating the attack of the Mist Demons. As for the divine Phosphotex, I am sure that the author of *The Abolition of Thought* needs no words of praise from such as I.

"I suspected that Ganelon had emerged from one of the

rare Time Vaults because of the fact that the Ardelix
ruins lay in close proximity to that portion of The Barrens
in which you discovered him. The Hybrids of Phex vener-
ated the Time Gods and worshiped their wisdom, and
their city was situated thusly due to its propinquity to the
site of one of the Time Vaults. But Ganelon had emerged
in the mindless state which made him vulnerable to destruction by inimical forces; these were unlike the Time
Gods, who rarely take chances. Then I learned that a subterranean convulsion of nature had occurred beneath the
westernmost of the Crystal Mountains only a few hours before you found him wandering in the Barrens. A micro-
meteorite of pure yxium had penetrated the flanks of the
mountains unobtrusively, causing a mere pinprick. The
yxium did not vaporize until it struck the magma level far
beneath the mountains; yxium is a peculiar metal, found
only in the core of certain stars, which reacts to the gravitational field of a celestial body in a manner exactly the
opposite of other forms of matter: in a word, it falls *up* instead of down. The sudden discharge of yxium vapor
caused a temporary reversal of gravity at the mountain-
roots, affecting several million tons of earthweight. It was
this convulsion, undiscernible on the surface, which disrupt-
ed the Vault. It cracked open like an egg, thrusting Ganelon forth upon the world before his time."

"Why had the Time Gods not foreseen this
eventuality?" asked Phlesco, who was hardly able to keep
up with all of this.

The Illusionist shrugged. "I really cannot be sure. Perhaps they saw the future in a purely visual manner; as I
have said, the subterranean explosion was so deeply situated as to not even cause the slightest tremor on the surface. Now the bodies preserved in such Vaults are created
at full, mature growth, but their minds are blank. Clever
contrivances educated the supermen and superwomen by
telepathic induction; the termination of their educatory
phase is timed to coincide with the moment of their pre-
destined emergence. From the mindless condition of your
son when first you found him, I am forced to conclude that
Ganelon was not due to emerge from the Ardelix Vault for
quite some time; perhaps a matter of months, or years, or
even uncounted millennia. And I have not the slightest notion to suggest what future doom he was designed to prevent or, at least, to cope with. We may never know this."

"Then why is all of this suddenly so important?"

"A reasonable question. The Queen of Red Magic has this very day arrived in Zermish *to purchase Ganelon Silvermane from your local Hegemon.* I can only conclude from this data that she has discovered his true identity and that his continued existence is in some manner inimical to her plans. She is a wily, unscrupulous, ambitious, and malignant creature, and among other things she plans to incorporate all of the realms of North YamaYamaLand into an empire, with herself as empress."

"Do you suppose that this could be the future danger which Ganelon was sent here to prevent?"

"I don't know; but I don't think so. She has not as yet attained to sufficient power to bring her plans to fruition; we in this part of the world have as much to fear from the Ximchak Barbarians and their new, and dangerously brilliant, Warlord, as we do from Zelmarine."

"The *what* barbarians?"

"No matter; they have not yet arrived on the scene. Now, the Hegemon will sell Ganelon to the Red Queen—"

"How could he? I mean, a free citizen cannot be sold like a slave. Much less a national hero!"

"The Hegemon will not dare refuse; Zelmarine is too powerful. And he may do so under the law. Recall that Ganelon like the other militiamen, took the Oath, which makes him the personal property of Argelibichus, his to dispose with as he deems best. Yes, I know, the Oath was designed to prevent bereaved relatives of dead warriors from suing the Hegemon in the courts for reparations; however, it serves the same purpose as slavery. And the emergency has not yet been declared officially ended, or the militia dispersed, or the Oaths rescinded. As for Ganelon's being a national hero, well, Argelibichus will put the best face on it as always. He will say Ganelon has entered the service of a friendly neighboring monarch, to help her realm against some imaginary invasion or other, and that the grateful Queen has bestowed an immense treasure upon Zermish by way of saying thanks. He will claim Ganelon was swayed by motives of the highest degree of patriotism; something like that."

"Well, what's to be done, then?" grumbled Phlesco.

"Let me take him into my service; apprentice the boy to me. I am ready to depart upon the instant, and the papers are here in my pouch. But swiftly, swiftly! Time is of the essence."

Just then the door banged open and Slunth the haruspex stuck his scruffy head in the room.

"Friend Phlesco! A squadron of the Palace Guard are entering the district. It is said they have come to escort Ganelon to the Hegemonic presence. What's afoot?"

Phlesco's eyes popped.

"Great Galendil, you're right! Quick, where do I sign? Iminix, stop snuffling into that apron and bring the boy's war-gear—and don't forget the Silver Sword!"

9.

A HASTY DEPARTURE

While Iminix scurried to bundle together some garments for Ganelon, Phlesco the Godmaker signed the Deed of Indenture which made his adoptive son the apprentice of the Illusionist. Slunth the haruspex also signed the document as the outside witness demanded by Zermetic law. Then they were ready to depart.

"But, Father, I don't want to be a magician. I want to become a warrior."

"This is for your own good, you great lout! Now get along with you. Mind your manners, and see that you obey your master."

Ganelon sighed. "Yes, Father. Good-bye, Father."

Iminix sniffed loudly, wiping her nose on the damp apron. She did not hold with magicians; still and all, it was better than letting the boy fall into the clutches of that red minx with her high-and-mighty airs. There was no telling what a woman of such doubtful morals and questionable character would be doing to a simple, innocent lad like Ganelon.

"Take this," she said, thrusting a bundle into his hands. "You will be hungry on the way, I'll warrant. No telling what you men will have to eat in that lonely palace, with no women around to cook for you. Well, just remember to dress warm and wear your galoshes when it rains."

"Yes, Mother. Good-bye, Mother."

"See that he gets to bed at a decent hour, now. A growing boy needs his sleep. And don't let him strain his eyes, reading all those books of yours, and in a poor light, too, I imagine."

"I will, madam," said the Illusionist, mastering his impatience. "He will be well cared for, I assure you. Now we really *must*—"

"Here is a bottle of my special cough medicine; see that he takes it if he gets a cold. And here is a packet of my herb tea; try to see that he drinks a cup every night, just before bed. It is so good for the stomach. This salve is the best thing I know for a rash, in case he—"

"Soldiers coming down the street!" Slunth squeaked from the doorway. The Illusionist nodded, stuffed the herbs and medicines Iminix was pushing into his hands into Ganelon's duffel, and taking the bewildered giant by the arm, shoved him toward the rear door that opened into a tiny backyard.

"We really must be going now," he said hastily.

"Go with Galendil, boy. Try to be a good boy, now!"

"I will try, Father. Good-bye, Father! Good-bye, Mother! Good-bye, Master Slunth—"

Swearing under his breath, the Illusionist pushed Ganelon into the huge transparent bubble of steel-strong glass he had parked in the backyard, sealed the door, tossed Ganelon's gear to the curved floor, and made the bubble float up out of the patch of grass and over the rooftops. It moved sluggishly, due to the extra weight of the youthful giant, who weighed somewhat more than two grown men.

"Won't the Hegemon be angry with my father, letting me get away, and all?" the young giant asked, worriedly.

"No, there will be no trouble from that direction," the Illusionist said with conviction. "He will assume your apprenticeship the result of an unfortunately mistimed coincidence, nothing more. Since there would have been no way Phlesco could have known what was happening at the palace, or of his acquiescence to Zelmarine's demands. Your father, as a leading Burgess, is too important a member of the municipal government for the Hegemon to wreak vengeance upon. I know the man—that is, I know his predecessors, which is the same thing."

Staring down at the rooftops and towers as they glided by beneath the crystal floor, the giant asked: "What about this Queen of Wherever-it-is, then. Won't she be mad with Father?"

"No, you can rest easy there, as well. She deems herself above such sentiments as vengeance. She will merely bide her time, hoping to get you into her toils at a later date. Everything will be all right, Ganelon; leave it to me."

Ganelon said nothing. He was watching the city recede into the distance as the bubble of tough glass floated across the Plains of Uth toward the mountains. Perhaps he was saying good-bye to Zermish, the city wherein he had spent his youth, the only city he had ever known. Or perhaps he was remembering the mighty battle that had been fought and won on these very plains, not long ago. It was impossible to tell what he was thinking from his expression.

"Where are we going?" he asked, after a little time.

"To Nerelon, of course. That is the name of my palace."

"Where is Nerelon?"

"In the mountains, naturally. You must stop asking me questions for a while, Ganelon, for I am having trouble trying to keep this *nembalim* aloft. You are too heavy for it; it is a two-man craft, and our combined weight must be at least that of three, nearly four."

"What is a nembalim?"

"This thing we are flying in!" snapped the Illusionist. He was beginning to understand why Phlesco had always been so short tempered with the boy, and fancied him a bit of a simpleton. Then, striving for patience and remembering that an apprentice must ask questions in order to learn anything, he said, 'more calmly: "This form of aerial contrivance was popular in my youth. They were made by the Fabricators of Dirdanx, a race of artisans in Quentland, now extinct, I believe. They are called *nembalim*, singular, *nembal*, plural. It is a curiosity of Quentish."

"What is?"

"The word endings, you great idiot! Quentish is a language invented by the trebly-cursed Dirdanxmen, who refused to speak anybody else's language, insisting on one of their own." He simmered down, mastering his temper. Then, as an afterthought, he added, absently: "I had this one as a gift from King Wuntho, payment for a favor or two."

"Who is King—"

"The King of Quentland, you fool! Who else? Now hold your tongue while I try to lift this cursed thing over those filthy foothills, will you?"

"Yes, master."

They were entering the Crystal Mountains by this time, having passed over the Warza and circling around Zaim Rock, the lookout point at which the Zermetic riders had been ambushed while trying to set afire the eastern edge of the Warza in order to slow the advance of the Indigons. Sunlight flashed and sparkled on the huge facets into which the Crystal Mountains were cloven. Ganelon admiringly explored them with his eyes. He had never seen the mountains from so close before. Or he could not remember having done so, for by this time he had long since forgotten having ever wandered in The Barrens; he had, of course, emerged from the Ardelix ruins in these same mountains just before Phlesco and Iminix had found him, but that had been before his mind had begun to form and he could not remember it.

The mountains rose to modest heights, few of them attaining to more than three thousand feet, and the range extended from the southwest to the northeast in an almost straight line for a distance of about six leagues. They were formed completely out of pure rock crystal, transparent as the finest glass, and were sheared into perfectly flat surfaces as polished and as regular as the facets of a jewel. Whether this was the work of nature or due to the labor of some race long ago forgotten in the backward abysm of time, no man could say. Probably they were natural formations. Nature was in flux in this Eon, and had been for several million years: new geological formations, like the Sky Islands; new kinds of matter, like the Trembling Land far to the west; and wholly new states of existence, like Antilife and Reality Flaws, were constantly coming into being. Perhaps that accounted for the Crystal Mountains; if not, no matter: there were many more curious mysteries in the vastness of Gondwane.

The foothills rose into the massif of the range itself, rank on rank of glass pinnacles, marching into the sunset. As the luminance of the westering sun caught the peaks with colored fire, shimmering chords and arpeggios of shade and tone spread through the interplay of self-mirroring surfaces, until the entire range blazed with incandescent glory. Pink, scarlet, purple, gold, canary yellow, dim green, metallic indigo, raw orange—shades and permutations of color so complex or so subtle that Ganelon had no name for them—the range flared with splendor. it was a nightly miracle, the sunset transformation of the mountains; from Zermish it was a blaze of flickering fire, like an earthbound aurora, seen every night to the southwest. But never before had Ganelon seen it so close.

"Well, thanks be to Galendil! I was beginning to fear this old nembalim would prove unequal to the task," the Illusionist groaned. The bubble, waffling from side to side sluggishly, lifted itself over the crest of a mountain peak and wobbled to a landing in a cup-shaped depression in the glittering rock.

"Are we here, then, master?"

"We're nowhere else, my boy. Take all your gear with you, now. . . ."

"But where is Neleron?" asked Ganelon in a bewildered tone of voice, peering about puzzledly. Save for themselves and the glass globe, the peak, which was trimmed off into a plane exactly horizontal to the surface of the Earth, was empty except for mists that went whipping by, scudding before a wintry wind.

"*Ne*relon. You can't see it because it is invisible. Follow me, and watch your step! The wind is fierce at this height, and the stuff underfoot is as slippery as glass."

The Illusionist did something which caused a panel to spring open in one side of the sphere. Cold, dry wind smote them in the face. The robed form of the older man blocked the portal, his garments aflutter like the wings of maddened bats in the icy gale; then he hopped down to the sheer plane of crystal, lost his balance, skidded a bit, cursed, stopped himself, looked back, and gestured impatiently for Ganelon to follow.

Laden with his gear the giant climbed somewhat clumsily out of the bubble and clumped down to the glassy peak. He noticed that the stuff of the peak was scored with millions of tiny scratches. He wanted to ask what had caused these minute markings, but remembering that his master seemed not to like him asking so many questions, resolved to postpone the query. (He learned later that the winds, carrying grains of sand from the Voormish Desert west of the mountains, and blowing steadily for ages across the peaks, had been the cause of the scratchings.)

The Illusionist was trudging, half bent over from the wind, across the peak to a very misty spot toward its very center. Ganelon shouldered his duffel and followed him. The footing was indeed slippery, but the wind was not strong enough to bother Ganelon, who at this period weighed nearly four hundred pounds.

As he approached the misty region he saw a tall, towering structure slowly come into view. It was gray and nebulous at first, but gradually it resolved itself out of the mistiness. First it was only a blur on the retina, then a shadowy blot, and finally it took on substance and solidity and became a building.

At the entrance he paused to admire the marvel. Even seen from close up, the stone (or whatever it was) from which the palace was made was peculiarly difficult to see. His eyes seemed always to be sliding off it to look somewhere else. It was a grayish—no, a bluish ... no, an amethyst—well, it was really no color in particular. And it was partly transparent, or translucent; blurry around the edges, and the details seemed always to be changing just a little, always in motion.

The fact that it was hard to see it clearly was an illusion. And Ganelon got an inkling of what it meant to be an Illusionist.

"Come in, come in, you lummox! Let me close the door against the wind before we freeze—you can gawp later, all you wish!" fumed the Illusionist. Ganelon entered, carefully wiping his huge feet on the top step before crossing the portal—his mother had always insisted on this—and helped the magician push the great slab of a door firmly shut against the gale.

"Fryx? Fryx! Where are you, lazybones?"

Here, master, a small voice answered within Ganelon's head.

"Hot water in basins, you rascal; scented towels, and mulled spice-mead and meat cakes in the Great Hall! And light the fire, too. Use the earthenware mugs, mind you!" commanded the Illusionist, showing Ganelon where to park his gear.

The giant turned about to see who Fryx was, and got the shock of his life. But even as he stared, he had a hunch it was going to be only the first of many such surprises, now that he was apprenticed to a magician.

10.

MORE ABOUT THE TIME GODS

The portal of the enchanted palace opened into a small vestibule; from this, a narrow passageway led into a huge stone-walled room whose lofty ceiling was supported by ten columns of veined purple marble of enormous girth, ranged in a wide circle. This was the Great Hall, obviously; there was a fireplace built against one wall, huge enough for six men to sit at table within it. The fireplace was of rich, glistening malachite of a virulent, poisonous green. Fryx, who had snapped out of existence a moment or two before, now snapped back. He pointed one limb at the fireplace, where immense tree trunks, cut into logs as big about as Ganelon's chest, were piled on andirons of glittering brass shaped like three-headed Flions. In obedience to his—or its—gesture, the logs burst into ruddy, crackling flames that flooded the room with light and warmth.

Heavily cushioned chairs stood about: at his master's request, Ganelon drew them up near the fender. Then he washed in the steaming water, basins of which had appeared when Fryx had, dried himself on thick, warm, perfumed towels, and sat down in one of the chairs. It had looked to be the sturdiest of all, but even it groaned alarmingly under his weight.

"Fryx, you rogue, where are those mugs and cakes—ah!"

They came floating unsupported into the room from some unseen doorway or aperture behind them, two mugs leaking steam and two platters of hot, delicious-looking cakes. They came parading up to the fire, separated into two sets, one of each, circled about, and deposited themselves gently, with just the faintest *click* of resumed weight, on benches drawn up by the chair arms.

"Help yourself, my boy," the Illusionist mumbled, chew-

55

ing hungrily. The spice-mead was much more alcoholic than anything Iminix had ever let him taste, but hot and bracing. The cakes were crisp and buttery, stuffed full of succulent scraps of tender beefy meat; Ganelon gobbled a handful, discovered they instantly replenished themselves, and gobbled more.

All the while, his eyes were following Fryx about the room, as the Illusionist's servant snapped in and out of existence, lighting candles taller than Ganelon himself, which were fixed on heavy platinum bases; bringing the Illusionist a bundle of sealed documents and scrolls in ivory tubes, and letters from which purple or scarlet ribbons dangled importantly—this would seem to be the Illusionist's mail that had accumulated during his absence. Ganelon could hardly take his eyes off the creature, Fryx.

"What is the matter, my boy?" the Illusionist asked, noticing Ganelon's fascination. "Haven't you ever seen a Gyraphont before?"

"Well, actually, no. I've seen pictures of them, though, in the Bestiary Father has. . . ."

"Hmm. That would be Phylith's *Compendium*, most likely. Yes, Fryx is a handsome specimen of his kind; I have always thought Master Phylith failed to do the *genus Gyraphontus* justice in his portraiture. Still and all, it hardly behooves me to criticize: can't draw a straight line, myself. More mead?"

"But aren't they, well, dangerous? I'd always heard. . . ."

"Dangerous is not the word, my boy. They're man-eaters, or soul-eaters rather; comes to the same thing, I suppose. Yes, but Fryx is not unintelligent, keeps himself personable; quite docile, actually; good-natured, even. Don't worry about him, Ganelon, he is bound completely to my will, as is everything and everyone you will find here at Nerelon. Nothing here can or will harm you, no matter what they might do to you in the outside world."

"I will remember that, master. Master, may I ask you a question?"

The warmth of the fire, or perhaps the spice-mead, had taken the edge off the Illusionist's temper. He nodded indulgently.

"Why did you save me from that Queen? Was it for me, or for yourself?"

The Illusionist looked at Ganelon with surprise. The youth was full of surprises, he was beginning to realize.

He was not as stupid as first thought. The question had been remarkably perceptive, even shrewd.

"Both, actually. I have nothing against you—in fact I rather like you—and I am certainly interested in you and in finding out just what you were designed for. Then again, I like your father and mother; they are fine people, and they would be hurt if anything happened to you. Also I am not friendly with the Red Queen, whose intentions I mistrust and whose ambitions I fear; I am anxious to keep you out of her hands because I am not certain why she wants to get you into them, and I do not know the uses to which she would put you. Then again, to be honest, I have certain things in mind that I want to do, and you can help me greatly in performing them." He paused, then added "And by the way, in case you were not sure, the manner in which I desire to employ you is honorable and will be for the good and safety and happiness of all men. I have no ambitions of empire, myself. I look upon myself, to some extent, as the protector of these parts of YamaYamaLand; there are forces at work in Gondwane this hour that would murder or enslave or pervert the ordinary people of these lands—the decent, law-abiding, Galendil-fearing people, like your mother and father. No one knows about these dangers yet, only I: but I intend to oppose them, and I hope to destroy them in time, with your help. But these things are still in the future, although coming nearer all the while; we shall speak of them at another time."

Ganelon digested this in silence. His heavy face was brooding, his fierce black eyes were thoughtful, even haunted. The Illusionist watched him quietly until he spoke.

"You told my father that I am a Construct. That means I am not a human being?"

"I don't know just how human you are, Ganelon. Because I haven't yet found out just what powers you have been given that are not possessed by ordinary men or women. But I suspect that, these extra powers aside, you are completely human in every important way, except that instead of being born you were made."

"That seems to me to be a very big difference."

"Perhaps it does seem so to you, but I don't think it matters much," The Illusionist said kindly.

"You don't know why I was made, or what I am supposed to do?"

"No, I don't. That is one of the things we shall have to

look into. Maybe, when we have discovered just what powers you have been given, we can deduce from them what sort of deed or exploit you were designed to perform; I don't know. I hope so, for I believe it is tremendously important for us to know this. All I do know is this: you were put together in such a way that you are supposed to save the entire world from some peril or doom that threatens it, or will threaten it."

Ganelon ruminated on this for a bit, then spoke up with another of those surprisingly intelligent insights that the Illusionist was beginning to respect.

"Maybe I am supposed to fight those forces you said were threatening these lands."

"That's a very intelligent guess. But I don't think so; I am myself strong enough to deal with them, or such is my opinion, anyway—although I will be grateful for your help in those matters. No, these are merely local troubles I am going to deal with: you were sent to help the whole world from some impending doom that threatens all men, everywhere."

"How can you know that for certain?"

The magician laughed behind his veil of lavender mist. "My dear boy! I know hardly *anything* for certain: that is supposedly the first step toward true wisdom. I hope so! But, no, Ganelon, really. The only other time we know for sure that the Time Gods sent a Construct into the world it was to save Grand Velademar; in so doing, Calidondarius saved the entire world, that is to say, the Future of Man. Such as it is."

Ganelon wrinkled his nose. "Cal . . . Calidon—?"

"—darius; better known as the Thinker of Aopharz. Did your father ever teach you about him?"

"I don't think so. But there's a statue of him in the square before the Hegemon's palace. A diorite statue, very big; bigger, even, than the one of the First Hegemon."

"Quite right. Without him, there wouldn't have been any First Hegemon, or anything else, today. You see, there was once a time when all of human civilization had been reduced to one small country, the Thirtieth Empire it is called. It was almost the Last Empire, because except for Grand Velademar all the rest of Gondwane was a savage wilderness where dangerous beasts and wild, uncivilized Nonhumans fought each other for supremacy. When the Thinker was released from his Time Vault, at a place called Aopharz, the end of the world was only a thousand years away. A barbarian horde was arising in Farj and Quonseca; in time it would sweep across Gondwane, trampling the Thirtieth Empire into the dust, slaying or enslaving the last True Men. This could have been the extinction of mankind; at very least, it would have meant the end of our civilization. But nobody knew the Green Jehad was coming, or that the terrible Urghazkoy Horde was forming. Nobody in the world knew. But the Time Gods knew. They had known it ages before. They were long since dead themselves; but they had left a superman sleeping in the Aopharz Vault to deal with that peril, when it arose."

"What did this Calidondarius do, exactly?" asked Ganelon.

"Nothing very important. He was no warrior, no strong man like you. He was a scholar, what used to be called a 'scientist,' when there was such a thing as science, before the laws of nature started to change, and the world to change with them. He kept a science from dying, that's all. He kept three books alive; he taught young people the science called solesmic bionomaly; that's all. Nobody alive today even knows what that term represents, or what that strange science was supposed to do. But, long after the Thinker himself was dust, a thousand years later when the Green Jehad moved across the breadth of Gondwane from south to north, destroying everything in its path, enough people still knew how to use solesmic bionomaly, to stop the Urghazkoy."

"What did they do?"

The Illusionist went over to the wall in which there was, quite suddenly, a window, or what looked like a window. Through it the enormous silver rondure of the Falling Moon glared down at Old Earth. He pointed.

"There they are, the Urghazkoy. They must be very far beyond the Moon by now, halfway to Mars maybe, or entering the asteroids."

"But *how*—"

The Illusionist shrugged and yawned; he was getting a trifle sleepy.

"Nobody knows. But when the Horde swept down the valley to ride against Grand Velademar, last of the human civilizations, they rode . . . *elsewhere*, instead; and they are still riding. . . ."

Ganelon looked at the Moon.

Suddenly he felt cold and alone and very frightened. Frightened of what? He did not know. Frightened, perhaps, of what was someday to come, when he should stand against doom and strive to save the world from something he did not understand.

11.

FRYX, AND OTHER ODDITIES

Next morning a cold horny claw against his bare shoulder brought Ganelon suddenly, jarringly awake.

Master say you wake up now, a thin voice said tinnily in his brain.

It was Fryx, the Illusionist's tame Gyraphont. The tall jointed thing turned away, bent to light the fire in Ganelon's room, and began laying out his garments before the blaze.

Ganelon climbed out of bed and went to relieve himself in the closet-sized little cubicle which the Illusionist referred to as "the sanitary facilities" but which the young giant thought of as "the jakes." He hadn't got the various faucets and plugs straightened out in his mind and nearly scalded himself, but Fryx came to his rescue.

This for hot, this for cold, this for flush-um, said Fryx.

Ganelon nodded, trying to remember it all. He bathed and emerged to don his warrior's harness, finding instead a capacious gownlike thing with deep pockets and flapping sleeves, colored a revolting lilac.

"Hey, Fryx! I can't wear this thing—where's my other gear?" he demanded of empty air.

Fryx popped back into sight again and looked at him severely. There were thirteen eyes in all, which made being stared at by a Gyraphont rather unsettling.

Master say you wear, so you wear. Other stuff put away, said Fryx, and vanished again. Ganelon got into the hideous lilac robe unhappily, and went down to breakfast with a gloomy look. The magician, wrapped in a snuff-colored robe, a stocking cap adorning his pate, and carpet slippers on his feet, was already working his way through a stack of buttery giffcakes dripping with syrup, with a half-demolished platter of sausages at his elbow. Despite the informality of his attire, his visor of lavender mist was already in place; Ganelon wondered moodily if he slept in it.

Breakfast was served by invisible hands, and at the size of the repast, Ganelon's spirits rose somewhat.

"No work today, my boy; a little tour of Nerelon first, to acquaint you with your new home. Hurry up and finish that second helping and we'll be off."

The palace contained many more rooms than was strictly possible, considering its apparent size as seen from without, and the rooms were much larger than they could have been. But Ganelon didn't bother his head about that: there were too many curious and interesting things to look at. There was a room filled with books, ranked in rows from floor to ceiling, along the walls, and even above the doors and over the windows. Some of them were bound in colored cloth and some in vellum, others in lizard-hide or serpent-skin or dragon-leather. One enormous tome was bound in the green fur of a Great Horned Wuz, and others were between boards of carved wood, sheets of metal, plates of ivory, and so forth. There were more books in that room than Ganelon had ever seen or heard of, more, in fact, than he would have believed the world contained.

Many, if not most, of the volumes were heavily enchanted. The Illusionist showed him one written in a completely forgotten language, undecipherable by any living man. The Illusionist had cast a spell upon it, however, and the book read itself aloud when opened.

"Try it, my boy," the magician urged affably. "Just open it anywhere."

Ganelon gingerly opened the volume to a page midway through. A quiet, confidential voice began speaking in a neutral tone of voice.

" . . . Page 407. In all other respects the Ninety Sigils of Sgandru may be employed as defenses against the inhabitants of the Fourth Plane. When displayed in conjunction with the enunciation of the ritual called the Pearl of Great Price, with the Star Jashera in the ascendant, a defense may be erected which is proof against the Dwellers in the Moon House, although in this respect it is wise for the karcist to recall the warnings of Dng the Conjuror, that the Moon House spirits are subtle and cunning and will strike when the ritual has been finished, biding their time until that moment. The ninety-first sigil, sometimes credited to Sgandru, is believed a forgery added to the canonical Ninety by the renegade sorceror Langarch of Oym ..."

Ganelon closed the book hastily and the soft voice was cut off abruptly.

"This is my Consultarium," said the Illusionist, ushering the young giant into a small chamber draped in yellow satin. On small pedestals ranged about stood skulls, mostly human, the heads of mummies, and several artificial heads of stone, lava, wood, brass, and silver. The eyes of these sculptures were inset with crystals which gleamed with watchful intelligence in the light of dim ruby lamps.

"Each of these heads is the receptacle of a spirit with whom I may wish to converse on vaious matters," said the magician casually. "That mirror of black steel on the wall to your left imprisons a djinn from the planet Yingg who is particularly knowledgeable on astral and etheric plane matters."

A full-length suit of fantastic armor, made of the blue metal called nthium, stood in one corner. When the Illusionist addressed it the metal creature creaked into life and motion.

"Hail, master!" boomed a hoarse voice from within the empty helm. Ganelon jumped as the thing saluted with a lifted arm.

"Calm yourself, my boy. This is my favorite automaton, a tireless war-machine of limited intelligence. When venturing into a dangerous region I generally let Azgelasgus accompany me. His metal strength has saved my skin on more than one occasion."

"Azgelasgus?"

"Yes, I named him after the famous hero of legend; he is every bit as brave, and probably several times stronger."

They passed on. There were several other automatons, some made of glass or porcelain, designed to be resistant to acids and corrosive vapors, which assisted the Illusionist in his alchemical experiments.

Against one wall a shadow moved without anything to cast it. The magician addressed it and the shade replied in a thin, faint voice like fingernails scratching against slate.

"This is a wraith called Vloob, whom I consult on transmundane matters. Vloob, this is my new apprentice, Ganelon, called Silvermane."

"My full name is Vloob Atz, young man," said the ghost. Ganelon greeted it halfheartedly.

"I rescued him from the Thirty Scarlet Hells of the Eshgòlian mythology; he had been damned an age or two earlier by the Zealots of Jashp, who formerly inhabited the Moving City of Kan Zar Kan. That was one of the Robot Cities with which the Technarchs of Vandalex briefly experimented."

"Are you happy, being a wraith?" Ganelon asked, curious.

"I suppose so," the wraith replied tartly. "Are you happy, being a Construct? At least, I am happier here than in my former state. There are worse things than ghosthood, young man! Unfortunately, the Afterlife as envisioned by the Zealots does not include a paradise, or even a limbo: nothing but a succession of hells, each more uncomfortable than the last. I would rather be here than where I was when G—"

"*No names!*" the Illusionist said sharply.

"—when the Illusionist rescued me," the wraith finished lamely.

They came to a glass-roofed garden filled with peculiar trees. They were carved of crystal, those trees, congeries of graceful, curving stems which burst in swaying sprays of jeweled fruits—lavender, mauve, amethyst, gray-green, dim purple.

Perfumed winds blew constantly through the enchanted gardens, making the crystal branches sway and causing the jeweled fruits to ring together, a weird, ghostly music, like wind-chimes.

The grass was rustling blades of sparkling silver. Small streams of bright red and golden fluids ran gurgling. Flowers of blown glass, tinted in rare pastels, nodded in the breeze.

"I built this garden to remind me of my homeland," the Illusionist said dreamily. Ganelon stared at the garden.

"It is very beautiful," he said. "You have never mentioned your homeland before. Is it far away?"

The magician glanced at the sky, which had suddenly

darkened to dim purple and was abruptly thronged with glittering stars. He pointed at a brilliant star of zircon-yellow.

"The second star to the right," he said strangely. "A star called Froynox; very faint and difficult to see."

Ganelon regarded him with astonishment.

"Do you mean you are from ... another world?"

"From the seventh planet which revolves about Froynox, or which used to, anyway. I was a magician there, in a former life. The people of Froynox have a custom, hallowed by ancient tradition. When a personage of rare and unusual distinction dies, they extract his subtle essence from his brain, encase it in a minute grain of imperishable crystal, and propel it into the depths of space with a vacuum cannon. There he wanders betwixt the stars forever. In my case, however, the essence of my former self, encysted in crystal, fell to Gondwane in a meteor shower, was absorbed into the roots of a Dargowany tree. My Earthly mother ate of the fruit of this tree and the grain of crystal entered into her womb and became a part of her unborn child—which was my present self."

The Illusionist mused. "In time I was born again and entered into training at the School of the Sixty Sciences in Nembosch. During my novitiate one performs the ceremonial termed 'The Opening of the Gates,' in order to relive past lives and learn therefrom. Thus I came suddenly into full possession of my former memories of Froynox, which included a knowledge of all the magical sciences. It was in this peculiar manner by which I became what I am today, a thaumaturge of vast learning, authority, and power. ... Do you believe this story?" he asked suddenly.

Ganelon blinked. Then he said, slowly: "I am not sure. It is unlikely; but it is not really impossible, I suppose."

"Do you trust me to tell the truth?" the Illusionist pressed.

"I suppose I do—on large and important matters, at any rate. On matters of small consequence, I believe you might well fabricate a hoax or an imagined anecdote by way of joking, or to amuse yourself in a moment of boredom."

"And do you consider this Froynox tale to be of small consequence?"

"Yes, I think so."

"Why?"

"Because it has no genuine bearing on our present condition or our future course of action, at least none that I can see."

The magician looked at him for a long time in silence.

Then he said: "You delight and amaze me, Ganelon. You are learning to think; I am impressed with that." He gestured: stars cleared from the sky, whose dull purple brightened back to noontide brilliance. "Come; it is time for lunch."

Ganelon followed obediently.

But he noticed that the Illusionist neither admitted nor denied that he had lied about his ultratelluric origins. And never at any later time did Ganelon learn the truth of the story.

12.

CONVERSATIONS WITH VLOOB ATZ

His new life at Nerelon soon settled down to routine. In the morning he exercised his strength before breakfast. In the forenoon he partook of certain experiments with the Illusionist which were designed to explore the nature of his powers. After lunch he was free to wander, explore, or otherwise amuse himself just as he wished. During the hours between lunch and dinner the magician closeted himself in his sanctum, busied with matters that bore no direct relation on the mystery of Ganelon Silvermane.

It was not as lonely a life as it sounds. Ganelon was by nature amiable and easy-going, even sociable. He lost his fear of such weird creatures as Fryx the Gyraphont, Azgelasgus the automaton, or the wraith of Vloob Atz. He made friends with them, after a fashion, and with the curiosities in the menagerie of marvels that occupied one entire wing of the Illusionist's palace.

Among these was a Youk which had been given quasihuman intelligence and even the gift of speech. The immense, spider-limbed thing, clad in an integument of slick, glistening fur, told him many strange tales of the jungled regions of Ongonoga from which it had been captured by hunters.

There was also a river-nix among the creatures in this weird zoo. The Nonhuman aquatic girl had a lissome, mostly transparent body and long green hair, thick and coarse as seaweed. Her face and torso were quite human, however, and even attractive. If you could overlook blue lips and nipples, and gill-slits in either side of her neck. Her name was Alyx.

The Youk and the Flion and the Sky Serpent were happy enough in their captivity, but Alyx pined for her native river, its secluded shores and deep pools, and for the companionship of her eighty-four sisters.

The Flion was named Rowrnor. It was a large, shaggy-maned, lionlike beast with rich orange fur and friendly, intelligent eyes yellow as pieces of topaz. Two sets of yellow-feathered wings grew from its body, one set from the burly shoulders, the other from the fat haunches. Sometimes Ganelon was permitted to exercise the Flion in the windy heights above the palace; on such occasions the winged flying lion was tethered to an unbreakable magic bridle, one end of which was sealed to a perdurable column of brass.

The Sky Serpent was named Jebd. It was vaporish and mostly insubstantial, and its kind lived above the clouds, where they slithered among the rainbows and fed from pure ice crystals in the stratosphere.

The Youk had no name.

Ganelon's best friend at Nerelon was the ghostly Vloob Atz. The wraith loved to talk, and waxed voluble on every conceivable subject. Ganelon asked him how he liked his spectral state of existence and, shrugging gossamer shoulders, the shade replied: "Not bad, all things considered. You neither hunger nor thirst, nor do you become weary and require rest or sleep. From neither heat nor cold do you suffer; you feel no emotion strongly, only, as it were, the echo of emotions. Time passes in a dreamy haze. It is very restful, lazy, contented. And it is enormously more pleasurable than spending a few million years in hell, I assure you!"

From time to time Ganelon assisted his master in certain expeditions. Once they flew in the glassy sphere to

Yembar Chasm, where the giant lowered the hollow metal figure of Azgelasgus on a heavy chain into the vertiginous deeps of the abyss. There the metal man gathered green fungi which sprouted from the bones of a monster's skeleton. The sides of Yembar Chasm were glittering vertical planes of lucent crystal. Within the glassy depths, weird figures flitted between the mirrorlike internal rifts and planes. Some of these came close to the outer surface of the chasm and yeeped and yammered soundlessly.

"Ghost-Phexians," said the Illusionist. They were towering green shapes, which flitted about on elongated nude limbs. Their flat heads were featureless, save for immense, drooling maws and great glowing eyes like sick yellow moons.

"Can't they come at us here?" inquired Silvermane.

The magician shook his head. "All planar surfaces in the regions which I often visit have been coated with an impenetrable transparent paint through which the Phexians are unable to gain passage. Were it not so, they would be all over you in an instant, sucking the marrow from your bones."

"How can anything immaterial enough to pass through solid crystal possibly suck my marrow?" Ganelon asked, doubtful.

The Illusionist laughed. "You really are learning to think, my boy! The answer is: they can't, of course. But they can make you think they are, because they can touch your mind. The thought that the gaunt, glowing things were sucking out your marrow would drive you mad. That would give them pleasure."

"How?"

The magician shrugged. "Who knows? They are all mad themselves. Perhaps misery likes company."

The fungi gathered, Ganelon bent his powerful arms to the task of drawing the automaton up out of the abyss. They left Yembar Chasm in the nembalim, which wobbled erratically from time to time. Mooring the vehicle in its circular hollow, the Illusionist touched the surface of the sphere thoughtfully. The glassy substance was clouded and lusterless, webbed with hairline cracks.

"I fear the globe has reached the end of its usefulness," he sighed. "It was never designed to cope with such weight as yours. Soon we shall have to seek some other mode of transport, or stay at home in Nerelon."

That night, chatting with the friendly wraith, Ganelon mentioned the Ghost-Phexians.

Depraved specters!" Vloob Atz sniffed disdainfully. "No decent, civilized apparition would dream of sucking marrow. It is a loathsome and despicable habit! I fear you are not being exposed to the most wholesome influences, child."

"I suppose not," said Ganelon. "Still, it's an education."

Another expedition followed this one to Yembar Chasm a few weeks later. The nembalim still had energy stores sufficient to carry the Illusionist, but he no longer dared risk transporting Ganelon.

"I dislike letting you go out unattended, master!" the giant protested.

"Nonsense, my boy. I still have my magic, and can call Fryx to me in case of need. But I must gather thunderbolts atop Mount Droom in order to vitalize my newest vat-creature. Tend to your lessons while I am gone, and don't get into mischief."

Ganelon nodded reluctantly; the magician left in the glassy globe, which went wobbling off in an erratic manner. The giant returned to his studies; the Illusionist had taught him grammar and punctuation. Now he was learning to cipher.

He was puzzling over his arithmetic problems when Fryx snapped into existence.

"Hello, Fryx. What's twelve times twelve?"

No know, the Gyraphont said hurriedly. *You come!*

"I'm to stay here and do my lessons."

The lobster-man clicked his fore-main-upper pincers before Ganelon's nose with a nasty *snikk*.

You come. Help master. Quick-quick!

"What's wrong with master; is he hurt?" said Ganelon, rising to his feet.

No hurt, no. Stuck. Sky ball no good no more. No can come home. Nice boy come along Fryx, quick-quick!

Ganelon tossed aside his slate and began putting on his boots. "I'll need my war-harness. And don't forget my sword!"

Hokay, me fetch. Fryx popped out of sight, returning a moment later with the leathern girdle, torso harness, and war-kilt. The swordbelt of the scabbard was looped about his scorpion-sting.

Ganelon ripped off his robe, a lime-green one this time, and began belting his nude body into the harness, buckling the heavy straps under his arms and across his deep chest.

Nice boy, good boy, you come quick now?

"What's up?" Vloob Atz screeched eerily, his shadow appearing against the tapestried wall.

"I don't know; the nembalim is inoperable, and I must go help the master."

"Don't let anything happen to him, or I'll be left with no one to talk to but those empty-headed automatons," said the wraith, worry in his scratchy voice.

"I'll do my best. Fryx, where is this Mount Droom, anyway? Will I have much climbing to do? Because in that case I'll need spike boots and a hook-staff. . . ."

The Gyraphont rasped his mandibles together in an agony of impatience.

No time for climb. You come along Fryx now—take hold! he said, extending one of the huge central-thorax claws. Ganelon eyed it dubiously; the pincers were big enough to snip him in half.

No be scared; Fryx no hurt. Come, come!

Ganelon swallowed, consigned his safety to Galendil's keeping, and clasped "hands" with the lobster-thing. They both vanished from sight.

"You go ahead; I'll keep the home fires burning," the wraith said encouragingly. Behind him, Azgelasgus came clanking into the chamber.

"What wrong, wraith? Trouble afoot? Best I trot out my trusty ax and charge off to the rescue!" boomed the metal man. Vloob Atz eyed him sourly.

"You get back where you belong, bucket-head, before somebody decides to use your body for a coal scuttle! *I'm* in charge around here when the humans are away. Get along with you now, before I give you a case of the seven-year rust—"

The automaton backed out of the room grumbling hollowly.

Ganelon and Fryx snapped into existence near the crest of Mount Droom, to find the Illusionist perched unhappily atop the dead, lusterless sphere, ringed about by snapping yerxels. Seven or eight of them lay dead, their white-scaled carcasses singed and blackened by miniature thunderbolts.

"Took your time, didn't you, Fryx?" the Illusionist said

wryly as they appeared. He had used up all but three of the thunderbolts he had been gathering that afternoon, and the yerxel pack still had thirty-five members left. They had elongated saurian snouts like dwarf alligators, and three wicked red eyes. They stank of iodine. Ganelon uttered a war-whoop and charged the lot of them, swinging the Silver Sword from side to side with vicious *whoof* sounds.

In no time he had cut three in half and crushed the skulls of four others. Hissing like a covey of teakettles they sprang upon him, but their claws could not get through the heavy leather straps of his harness to do anything more than merely scratch his tough hide.

Fryx vanished, reappearing immediately in the middle of the pack. Six or seven of his pincers snicked out to cut off heads, snouts, forelimbs, or whatever. They turned on him hissing furiously, but could inflict no damage at all on the Gyraphont. His scarlet chitin was proof to anything this side of steel needles.

The Silver Sword hummed vibrantly through the air, scattering a scarlet spray. Twitching yerxel corpses piled about Ganelon's feet. Before long, the pack, now considerably thinned out, decided to seek elsewhere for the evening meal, and the repulsive white reptiles vanished around a curve in the trail.

Ganelon helped the Illusionist climb down from atop the sphere. He thanked the Construct and the Gyraphont gruffly, angrily kicking the side of the sphere. The glass was completely opaque by now, and was beginning to crumble away to ash before their eyes.

"So much for the old nembalim! Ganelon, Fryx can only transport us one at a time. I'll go first, if you don't mind; I feel a little sick to the stomach. All that blood—ugh, the nasty brutes! Galendil must have been in a vile mood the day he invented yerxels."

Taking hold of the claw which Fryx first wiped clean on a dead yerxel, then extended to him, the Illusionist vanished. A few moments later Ganelon, too, returned to Nerelon. But the nembalim would never fly again; it shrank visibly, rejoining the elements of the air from which Fabricators of Dirdanx had solidified it, long ago.

13.

VITALIZING THE BIRD-MACHINE

It was two days after the disastrous expedition to Mount Droom; Ganelon and the Illusionist were seated in the Great Hall before a bellowing fire. Fryx lurked in the background polishing silver and careful to remain within earshot in case his services should be required. The wraith of Vloob Atz prowled among the folds in a wall hanging, humming to himself, and Rowrnor the Flion was stretched out on the hearth, wings folded, snoring like a gigantic dog. The Illusionist fretted and fussed with a tassel.

"It is really most annoying," he muttered. "By this time I had intended to be looking into conditions up north; I suspect that canny old devil of an Elphod has been making trouble for my friends the Tigermen of Karjixia. But since we can't fly . . ."

"The whatmen of where?" asked Ganelon.

The magician repeated the phrase. "You will recall I told you I foresaw three principal dangers that threatened these regions of Northern YamaYamaLand," he said. "The Queen of Red Magic is certainly one of them, and not the least of them, either; but we can safely set *that* problem aside until later. Then I had occasion to refer to the Ximchak Barbarians during a conversation with your father. This horde is still very far to the north and it will be years before they get down this far south; but they are coming, and when they get here, it will be touch and go to see if we can break them. They have recently come under the control of a Warlord of advanced military genius, and complete indifference to loss of human life. The combination is an explosive one. No, the most immediate hazard the inhabitants of Northern YamaYamaLand face are the Airmasters of Sky Island. Ever since the fanatic Vlydabec became their Elphod, or spiritual leader, I have feared for the lands to the north. I should have been there by now."

71

They ascended to the highest chamber of the palace, a ribbed vault whose windows lay open to the skies. Therein, reposing on the stone floor, lay a remarkable contraption. Ganelon stared curiously at it.

It was shaped like an enormous bird, sculpted from what appeared to be solid bronze, dark with age, and it was about thirty feet from parrot beak to spread peacock tail. The wings were also spread in a position horizontal to the body, and in that body an opening, like a cockpit, was hollowed out between the shoulders.

"What do you think?" asked the magician.

Ganelon remembered to close his mouth. "What is it? It looks like a Bazonga bird."

"Does it? Then that's what it is, I guess. This is a flying contraption invented by the late Miomivir Chastovix, a wizard who owned this palace before I did. Most of his equipment is still around here."

"You mean this contraption can *fly*? But it looks like solid bronze. If so, it must weigh tons."

The magician was amused. "It is; and it does. Or it would, were it not for the yxium crystals. Notice the way the metal sparkles? The bronze has been impregnated with ninety million particles of crystallized yxium. You will recall, I have spoken of yxium—the rare metal that reverses gravity, and is usually found only in the cores of distant stars."

Ganelon nodded somberly. "Yes; it was a meteorite of pure yxium that penetrated beneath the mountains and exploded there, cracking open the Vault; so, I believe, you said to my father."

"And so I did. Miomivir Chastovix was an alchemist of repute; he synthesized the stuff to pepper his bird-vessel with. The yxium particles completely offset the weight of the solid bronze, and the thing is slightly more than totally weightless. That's why I have it chained between the pillars, you see."

Ganelon examined the peculiar object with curiosity.

"Why, the eyelids are hinged, and so is the beak! And what is this machine in its throat, where the vocal cords would be on a man?" he inquired.

"A mechanical larynx," said the Illusionist. "Chastovix hollowed out the bird's head; notice the latches? The top of the crest opens—and set therein a sentient crystalloid. This is a form of crystalline life sometimes found in the

plains around Oth-Yom-Barqa, and the foothills there-
abouts. The crystalloids are mineral duplicates of the human
brain, with just as many internal electrical connections as
our brains have synapses, hence potentially as intelligent as
we are, except that they possess no senses or limbs."

"But why did he do this?"

"He intended for the bird-vehicle to fly itself, once completed. Those lenses duplicate the abilities of the human
eye adequately enough, and the vocal apparatus has been
connected to electrodes implanted in appropriate sectors
of the crystalloid brain. The bird-ears contain tympana as
sensitive to sound as our own eardrums."

"But the wings are solidly attached to the body—how
was the thing supposed to fly?"

"Energy storage crystals have been implanted in the
center of the body, connected to nexium tubes that run
the length of the torso and protrude under the tail. These
emit magnetic waves which my esteemed predecessor
believed sufficient to propel the vehicle. Other tubes
emerge from the front, from the wingtips, and elsewhere,
so that the contraption can turn and maneuver in the air.
It is all remarkably ingenious, in its way. Chastovix had a
gift for such mechanicals ... I hope!"

"It has never been flown, then?"

"Never even been tested. Never even been energized, or
vitalized, or whatever you call it. Miomivir Chastovix succumbed to the assault of a great mountain Youk before
completing the connections. I have perused his documents,
and believe that I can complete them."

Ganelon dubiously looked over the fantastic vehicle, but
said nothing. The Illusionist took up a sheaf of parchments
from a table and opened the bird's metal skull, lifting the
lid off by the topknot to expose the crystalloid, which was
nestled in a cushioning mass of spun-glass fibers. Of the
eighty-three copper electrodes, only four dangled loose.
Pausing from time to time to consult the alchemist's notes,
he carefully inserted the electrodes in place, and screwed
their caps on tightly. Then he stepped back.

"It should take a few moments to warm up, or whatever you call it," he murmured.

The bird's eyelids opened. That is, the metal caps fitted
over the vision lenses withdrew into grooves cut in the
bronze forehead. The lenses looked about, with an alert,
interested glitter that was most lifelike.

The hinged beak opened and shut a few times, creaking faintly.

"My, what remarkably ugly creatures!" marveled the bird, in a hoarse, squawking voice. "I suppose you are human beings?"

"Great Galendil, it speaks!" gasped Ganelon.

"Of course; before implanting the crystalloid in its braincase, Miomivir educated it in our language by reducing our vocabulary and grammar to a sequence of coded electrical impulses, which were then superimposed upon the sector identical with the human cortex. Tell me, bird," he said, raising his voice to address the creature, "do you know what and where you are?"

The brazen eyelids half lowered creakingly, lending the beaked face a dreamy expression.

"For ages untold I lay deep in the earth, with my brothers—or sisters, as the case may be. We could neither see nor hear nor feel; neither could we communicate. So we dreamed and thought and philosophized. Then a mighty convulsion raised us to the surface. This was when the continents came together, forming Gondwane . . . then we lay in the sun, absorbing energy; our impulses quickened; our mentalities became alert, stronger, more flexible. . . . Who are you humans, anyway?" the bird asked, suddenly breaking off its melancholy soliloquy.

"I am the Illusionist of Nerelon; this is my apprentice, Ganelon Silvermane."

"An unappetizing duo, if ever I saw one! But come to think of it, I have never been able to see before. And *my* name, what is it?"

"I'm afraid you do not have one," admitted the magician. The metal bird regarded him frostily.

"Nonsense! I am a sentient creature gifted with speech, even as yourselves. You have names; I deserve one too! What is it?" said the curious creature, with a disdainful sniff. The Illusionist opened his mouth to reiterate his previous remark, but Ganelon interposed hastily.

"You seem to have been fashioned in the likeness of a Bazonga bird," he said. The bird looked at him with interest.

"And what is a Bazonga bird, pray tell?"

"According to the Zul-and-Rashemba mythos, of which my mother was an adherent, it is a magical phoenix, divinely gifted with intelligence, which flies between heaven and earth, bearing messages from the Gods to their prophets, kings, and heroes. You bear a remarkable resemblance to the traditional representations of the Bazonga."

"Bazonga ... Bazonga," the bird-creature murmured rapturously. "My, what a singularly mellifluous name! So I am a Bazonga bird, then?"

"Not 'a'—'the.' For there is only one such creature in the universe; after ten thousand years of life it is devoured by an enormous mythological serpent called the Tzgàny, whose bowels become the womb from which it is reborn," explained Silvermane.

"We are wasting time with all this nonsense," grumbled the Illusionist. "What possible difference does it make whether the creature has a name or not?"

"It makes quite a bit of difference to *me*, I assure you," the Bazonga said primly. "Do you think I intend going through life being referred to as 'Hey, you!' or 'Birdie'?"

"Oh, very well, then," the magician said testily. "But let us get on with the testing; we have yet to ascertain if the vehicle can sustain the act of flight."

"Shall I—?"

"No, my boy! A fall from this height would kill even you; and I do not intend entrusting my old bones to the chancy winds. Descend to the Consultarium, will you; and bring my trusty Automaton here. He cannot be slain or destroyed, and any injury or damage can easily be repaired by just hammering out the dents."

Ganelon left the airy chamber, reappearing a few moments later accompanied by the clanking metal man.

"What ho!" Azgelasgus boomed nervously. "A flight aloft, what? Mayhap I had best postpone the adventure for a less windy day—"

"Get in the cockpit and stop worrying," commanded the magician.

"Of course; quite right! However, I have a slight case of rust in my left knee-joint ... perhaps tomorrow would be better?"

"Today will be fine. Get in, and no more of this nonsense!"

The metal man clambered gingerly into the front seat of the cockpit, peering about woefully. "Quite sure this contraption can fly, I suppose? I would be perfectly happy to forego the honor until further testing...."

"I am not a 'contraption,' you animated junk-pile; I am

a Bazonga bird, the only Bazonga bird there is in all the world," said the bird. Poor Azgelasgus jumped nervously as the vehicle addressed him in this manner, and tried to climb back out of the cockpit. A glare from the magician restrained him, however.

"I say! Talking vehicles . . . what next?" he complained doubtfully.

"Now listen carefully," said the Illusionist to the bird. "When I release your chains you will find yourself more than weightless. You will tend to bob skyward rather violently; to avoid smashing through my roof, you should be ready to direct a stream of magnetic waves against the roof, to hold you steady."

"Ah, yes," the bird marveled. "I am aware of my magnetic propellant-tubes . . . let me see, now . . . yes, I understand how they operate. An ingenious system, quite ingenious. Ready when you are, then!"

Upon the magician's order, Ganelon threw off the chains, releasing the Bazonga for flight.

"*Whoops!*" the bird squawked giddily, as it swung up toward the tower roof, then steadied, wobbling drunkenly from side to side; in the cockpit, the automaton howled dolefully, clutching the sides of the vehicle with his metal gauntlets.

Then, spying the huge open casements directly before it, the Bazonga activated its rear propellants and zoomed out of the window, tipping at a precarious angle. "And away we go!" sang the bird as it soared into uneven flight.

14.

THE FLIGHT
OF THE BAZONGA

From the window ledge, the Illusionist and Ganelon Silvermane watched as the ungainly metal creature zoomed about the tower in a drunken, wobbling curve.

"It doesn't fly terribly well," Ganelon observed after a time. The Bazonga had just gone careening past the window again, this time flying completely upside down, with Azgelasgus seated rigidly in the cockpit, visor squeezed shut so that he didn't have to see what was happening.

"Um," said the Illusionist. The bird had righted itself and was now executing a giddy sequence of figure eights, singing happily in a screeching voice while the poor automaton said, "Master? I say, Master! Make it stop doing that, won't you?"

Eventually the Bazonga learned how to maintain itself in an upright position during even the most hair-raising turns and aerial maneuvers. Finally the animated vehicle came floating back into the tower chamber, eyes shining with excitement.

"Did you see me fly?" the bird clacked excitedly. "Was I graceful? Did you see that last figure eight?"

"Very graceful," the Illusionist said sourly, "except when you were flying upside down. If you try anything like that while we are riding in the cockpit, I shall *de*vitalize you at the first opportunity."

The Bazonga came gently to rest in the original position. Azgelasgus, whose visor was still squeezed tightly shut, sat in his place as stiffly as a statue, and from time to time he said, faintly, "Master? Master? Are we down yet? Ho, there!"

"Ganelon, will you help him out of the cockpit? Bazonga, I am going to undertake an extended flight very soon, and want you to be ready to bear this youth and myself. So no unauthorized flights when we are not here, do you understand? Come, my boy, we have many things to do in preparation for our departure. . . ."

From his library the Illusionist procured a detailed chart of the regions about the country of the Tigermen; he studied this carefully while Fryx packed his gear for the trip.

"We will fly directly northwest, over the desert and beyond the country of the Death Dwarfs. The realm of the Tigermen lies beyond Holy Horx and Ixland, due west of Quay," the magician mused. "It will be quite a voyage, but I feel certain the Bazonga bird is capable of the exertion. After all, the creature has just been freshly vitalized and should not require new stores of energy for many months."

"Yes, master. I have packed my gear and my weapons.

When do you wish to embark?" asked Ganelon. The Illusionist shrugged.

"Now is as good a time as any," he said. "We can fly all afternoon, and will reach Horx by evening, with any luck. There we can procure sleeping cubicles for the night in a public hostelry; there are many such in the Hierophant's city, as it is a great center of pilgrimage."

Lunch plenty soon! Fryx said hastily.

"Well, right after lunch, then," the magician amended. The busy morning had left him with a hearty appetite. The Gyraphont set the table and served the Illusionist and his apprentice a delicious meal, which they tackled with gusto.

"Now, Fryx, while we are absent you must feed the beasts and do not forget to have Azgelasgus take the Flion out for his exercise at least twice a day, when the weather is good."

Fryx remember hokay.

"You must also tend to my vat-creatures, see that they have pap and water, and be careful that none of them escape from their restraints. Several of them are powerful enough to wreak considerable damage, were they to break loose, and none of them are yet sufficiently intelligent to obey my instructions, so it's up to you."

Fryx take care of them good.

"Well, then, I guess we are ready to go!" said the Illusionist, zestfully rubbing his palms together. "I will confess," he said to Silvermane as they climbed to the top of the tower, that I quite anticipate an enjoyable venture! I have not visited the Tigermen for some years now, and were it not for their present danger from the Airmasters, I should probably not venture into the jungle country for a decade. Ah, here we are! Well, now, bird, are you ready for departure?"

"Ready when you are," the Bazonga said amiably.

Fryx helped Ganelon store their luggage away in the tail-compartment of the articulate vehicle. The last bundle he stored carefully under the rear seat.

This lunch, the Gyraphont explained, *so you no get hungry on trip.*

"That's very thoughtful of you, Fryx," the Illusionist said. "But we shall be in Horx by nightfall, and will dine sumptuously, I am sure."

Just in case, maybe t'ings go wrong.

Ganelon helped the Illusionist into the cockpit, and climbed in beside him, storing his weapons on the unoccupied rear seat.

Take care you no get feet wet, the Gyraphont admonished anxiously. *Master dress warm, no get sniffles!*

The Illusionist smiled behind his veil of lavender vapor; the Gyraphont was as bad as Ganelon's mother had been, under similar circumstances. Still, it would not be kind to hurt the creature's feelings. So he solemnly reassured the lobster-devil he would keep out of drafts and see to the continued dryness of his pedal extremities.

Then, after a final farewell, the magician gave the word and the Bazonga zoomed out of the tower with a raucous screech of "Tally-*hoooo!*" And they were airborne at last.

The experience of flight was exhilarating in the extreme; it was also chilly in the extreme, the travelers soon discovered. All their previous voyages by air had been undertaken within the enclosed confines of the now inoperable flying glass bubble. Never before had the Illusionist realized quite how cold the winds could be; huddled in a fleece-lined cloak, whose hood was drawn up about his ears, the magician endured the frigid blast uncomplainingly. Yet he would not have denied that already he was looking forward with considerable gusto to a warm meal in a cozy hostelry in Horx that night.

They flew directly north. The glittering ramparts of the Crystal Mountains fell away, dwindling behind them. Beneath the Bazonga's keel—if a bird may be said to possess one—the plains grew sandy and desolate. Soon they were flying over the dreary expanses of the Voormish Desert.

It was quite late in the afternoon, the Illusionist realized. Already the old sun was a dimming red ball declining into the west. Far off to their left the lights of Abbergathy were a distant twinkling. Directly ahead of them the eastern extension of the Mountains of the Death Dwarfs rose upon the northern horizon. Far to the right, north of Zermish and Hegemonic cities, the Land of Red Magic lay.

There was still quite a considerable stretch of desert to be crossed before they reached the Country of the Death Dwarfs. The Illusionist consulted his chart through watering eyes. He thanked Galendil this was not the infamous

Gray Waste of Yan Kor they were traversing. That dubious region, far to the east of the Hegemony, was a thousand miles across; the Voormish Desert was only a fraction of its extent.

By now they must be halfway across the dreary waste of sterile sands; but they would be hard-put to reach Holy Horx by nightfall, he realized. Well, there was nothing to do but endure the flight with patience and fortitude.

Snuggling deeper into his warm cloak, the Illusionist dozed fitfully for a time. He was dimly aware of Ganelon seated by his side. Impervious to the windy cold, the young giant was chatting casually with their articulate mode of transport. The Bazonga was a voluble creature, and geography was a subject in which her alchemist-creator had not seen fit to tutor her. She had a thousand questions about the various lands and countries that spread about them, and Ganelon did his best to answer them with exemplary patience.

Sometime later, the Illusionist awoke from his doze with a rude start. It was quite dark by now, for the enormous luminance of the Falling Moon had yet to ascend over the world's edge to flood the stretches of Gondwane with its unearthly brilliance.

They were rapidly losing altitude, he realized.

"Why are we going down?" the magician demanded irritably.

"Because we are under attack," Ganelon said grimly.

Book Three

THE GREAT AIR MONOPOLY

The Scene: The Mountains of the Death Dwarfs; the Caravan-Camp; Holy Horx; the Country of the Tigermen; the Air Mines; Xombol.

New Characters: Voormish Nomads; Citizens, Priests, Guards, and Other Horxites; a Sirix of Jemmerdy; Tigermen, Death Dwarfs, and Air Miners.

15.

THE MOUNT LUZ AMBUSH

And so they were! Blinking his sleepy eyes open, the Illusionist stared about him in consternation. Quite obviously, they were engaged in crossing the mountains of Dwarf Country, for to every side rose sharp and jagged peaks of naked rock, pocked her and there with sparkling deposits of snow which gleamed bluely in the brilliance of the trememdous Moon.

These peaks were literally infested with little brutes, bald and squat and ugly, their leathery hides colored a poisonous shade of green. The yammering small uglies wore bits and pieces of iron but were mostly naked. They seemed utterly impervious to the cold winds, and were all curiously armed with hollow glass spears filled with a nasty fluid the Illusionist correctly guessed to be of venomous nature.

It would seem incontestable that the Death Dwarfs had somehow been apprised of their approach, and even of the route they would take in crossing over these mountains. For the shrilly squeaking little monstrosities had rigged an enormous net between two peaks, and into this net the Bazonga had innocently flown and was now entangled. This net, which was now draped about the head and neck and wings of the sentient vehicle, was composed of small-linked chains of steel rings, and was heavily weighted at the ends, which were fastened to great pieces of solid lead.

"I swear I never even saw the filthy thing," the bird squawked angrily. "One moment the passageway between these disgusting peaks was perfectly clear, and the next I was entangled in this vile net! But there was nothing in my way—nothing I could see!"

"Yes, yes, we believe you," snapped the magician. "No question of that, my dear Bazonga! The Death Dwarfs have recently come under the domination of our enemy, the Queen of Red Magic. It is quite within her power to foretell our route and to render this cursed net invisible until we blundered into it—"

The bird was sinking rapidly, weighed down by the heavy steel mesh. A hasty glance at the map told the magician they had been on their proper course; he himself had chosen to cross the mountains between the twin peaks of Mount Luz, hence there was no one to be blamed but himself.

The net, however, had proved insufficient to halt or to capture the Bazonga: there, at least, the Red Queen had erred! It was heartening to discover that their mysterious adversary was neither omnipotent nor infallible. Flying through the net, the Bazonga's speed had been powerful enough to rip it loose from its fastenings. Now the bird was sinking rapidly under the weight of the heavy steel chains; they were only three hundred feet above the sandy waste.

"I am doubling back into the desert country, you will perceive," the bird spluttered, clacking her beak furiously but unable to get her head clear of the clinging meshes. "It seems the only intelligent thing to do is to put as much distance between ourselves and those squeaking little devil-men as possible."

"Quite right, my dear Bazonga; very good thinking," muttered the Illusionist, his mind racing. "The Death Dwarfs fear and detest the Nomad caravans which dwell amid the Voormish, and are unlikely to pursue us here. Land anywhere you think best. Ganelon! Where is my bag?"

"In the tail-compartment, with the rest of the luggage, master."

"Curse it! All my instruments and magical devices are there. Well, there is no helping it; we'll unpack them when the bird has descended to Earth. . . ."

A few moments later the ungainly metal bird came floundering down to an awkward belly-flop landing amid the moonlit dunes. Ordinarily, the Bazonga would not have been able to actually bring herself down to the land surface, due to the upward impetus of her yxium crystals; but the heavy steel net that encumbered her far outweighed the antigravitic lift of the crystals.

The moment they came down, landing with a *whump* that shook the breath from the Illusionist, Ganelon clambered out of the cockpit and opened the rear compartment. They were in a pool of inky shadow cast by the crest of the dune nearby, and the light was insufficient for him to see clearly. He began rummaging through their luggage, looking for the magician's black bag of magic tools.

"Oh-oh! Watch it, you fellows," the Bazonga hissed warily. "We have company."

The Illusionist stood up in the cockpit so as to see over the bird's topknot. Then his heart sank into his boots, stayed there only a moment or two before rising to choke his throat.

Mounted on scarlet riding-lizards called *nguamodons*, a score of Nomad warriors sat watching them with impassive faces, tattooed bright purple.

From the gold rings in their ears and the tribal anchor-and-dolphin markings on cheek and brow, the Illusionist recognized them as the Azouk Clan of the Nomads of the Voorm nation. Luckily, this particular clan was friendly to travelers; indeed, to the Azouk Nomads, hospitality was a prime religious obligation.

With the assistance of the friendly Nomads, they managed to disentangle the steel mesh about the bird-vehicle, freeing the Bazonga from the clinging chains. Suddenly relieved of the burden, the metal bird bobbed twenty feet straight up into the air, before the creature could bring her weightless self under control.

This created quite an impression on the Nomads, as you might imagine.

"Ahoy! I see you are powerful sorcerors," said the leader of the Nomad party, a hawk-featured youth named Narosch. "The admiral will be delighted to extend to you the hospitality of the guest-cabin and a feast will doubtless be given in your honor. We are always pleased to have a sorceror among us, for they are closer to the Gods than the ordinary run of common men."

The Illusionist was flattered by this notion, which tickled his vanity. But he disliked having his plans set awry.

"That is extremely kind of you, Captain; but we had planned to pass the night in Holy Horx."

"That which has been planned can always be postponed." The purple-faced desert warrior smiled. "It is an old Voormish saying."

They were so far behind schedule by this time that they could hardly hope to reach Horx and procure sleeping cubicles before dawn; and the Voormish clans were proverbial for their hospitality. So it was decided they would accompany the friendly Nomads to their caravan-camp, which lay nearby. Ascending into the cockpit of the Bazonga bird once again, the Illusionist bade Narosch ride ahead with his entourage and show them the way. Then the bird-vehicle rose some thirty feet into the air and cruised after the loping scarlet reptiles and their sailor-like riders, forming a remarkable scene as they progressed over the moonlit dunes.

The Nomad clans regularly traversed the desert in wheeled caravans of landgoing ships. Some thirteen of these surprising vessels comprised the Azouk caravan; they were drawn into a ring with a huge bonfire built of lizard droppings ablaze in the center.

"Those wheeled carts look more like oceangoing vessels," said Ganelon, wonderingly.

"Essentially, they are," the magician explained as they alighted from their sentient vehicle and waited to be ushered into the ship of the desert prince. "Originally, the Nomads of Voorm were Sea Barbarians; but that was a couple of dozen thousand years ago. Since then the Inland Sea of Voorm has slowly receded, its waters seeping into cracks in the planet's surface. As the sea shrank, the dead sea-bottom took on the appearance of a desert. Gradually the Sea Barbarians became acclimated to desert life over many millennia; today they are wholly accustomed to Nomad life on the dry surface. However, ancient customs die hard among so tradition-bound a race, and their wains are still built in the form of the seagoing vessels their ancestors used ages ago to sail from island to island."

The prince of the clan, Ruascha (or the "Admiral," as he was called), was a lean and leathery man of advanced years. Vermilion rings were painted about his eyes; platinum hoops dangled from his lobes. His throne stood in the poopdeck cabin of the flagship, and in one gnarled hand he clutched the baton of his office, which was an antique spyglass of delicately carved narwhal-ivory.

"Ahoy, mates!" he cackled, greeting them with the immemorial salutation still employed by the desert dwellers. "Welcome aboard!"

They returned his greeting in the ritual phrase. He

waited until they were seated, then touched a gong. Slaves entered with smoking platters of tasty meats swimming in succulent sauces, carved wooden cups of spiced liquor, and desert vegetables cut in the shape of fish. While they feasted, members of the warrior clan performed a traditional hornpipe on the foredeck in their honor, while singing ancient sea chanteys.

After dinner the Illusionist entertained the company with an example of his powers. Setting out his instruments he lit green and purple powders in small pans over braziers of glowing coals, brought into play seven small, highly polished mirrors, and uttered thirteen words in an unknown language.

For a moment the Lost Ocean was reborn; sparkling green billows drove over the moonlit sands; sunlight flashed on the glistening forms of flying fish as they lazily went flapping by. The immense head of a Sea Unicorn broke the waves, striving to spear the aerial reptiles on the point of its ivory horn. The strong smell of salt and tar and fish rose to their nostrils; they could almost have sworn the deck swayed beneath them to the age-old rhythm of the tides.

Then the mirage faded, revealing dry sands extending in every direction, silver-blue under the radiance of the Falling Moon.

The admiral sighed in nostalgia for the days of his seagoing ancestors and politely thanked the magician for this example of the fine art of illusionry.

They spent that night in the guest-cabin. The wall-bunk was too small for Silvermane's gigantic frame, so after a cramped and sleepless hour, the young giant gathered up his bedroll and adjourned to the roof of the cabin where he slept out under the stars. Tethered to a zucca-zucca tree, the Bazonga bird floated nearby, crooning a song to herself while she awaited the return of day, when the two humans would awaken from the peculiar state they called sleep."

16.

HERETICS IN HORX

The Nomad clan was bound on a trading venture into the northern parts of the desert, where an ancient mesa rose several hundred yards above the dead sea-bottom.

Once the stone tableland had been an island called Oyj—that was in the days before the Voormish Sea become the Voormish Desert, of course—and the island city of Port Oyj had been a center of maritime commerce, much raided by the Sea Barbarians. The Oyjmen had resisted change in much the same manner as had the Sea Barbarians; they simply stayed at home, while the waters shrank and the former island became a mesa towering on its thick rocky spire far above the dead sea-bottoms. No longer was Port Oyj a merchant city, since it was difficult for anyone to conduct much trade with a city that now sat some twenty-one hundred feet in the air; but every year the former sea-raiders gathered at the foot of the mesa to recreate one of the ancient pirate raids. It was a festival enjoyed equally by the Nomads and the Oyjmen.

The Illusionist and Ganelon, riding in the Bazonga, floated along before the Nomad caravan for several leagues that morning until the Oyj mesa loomed upon the horizon. From this point they must part company with the friendly Azouks, in order to fly northeast to Horx. Ritual compliments were exchanged, and so were gifts, as was customary, Prince Ruascha presented Ganelon and the magician with examples of tribal handcrafts—carved bits of fossil-ivory scrimshaw. They in return presented their host with a few bright gems which had been set in the wingtips of the Bazonga by way of reflectors.

Then they circled the caravan of immense, wheeled ships, waggled their wings in farewell, and darted off into the morning.

The Mountains of the Death Dwarfs bulked near to the west; they were now well beyond range of any magics the vindictive little green monsters might hurl against them, said the Illusionist, and had nothing to fear.

Shortly before noon the walled stone city appeared beneath them. It was built entirely of a dusty, brick-red stone—that color being most pleasing to the Gods worshiped by the Horxites. The city was laid out in concentric circles, resembling an immense target. The main streets were circular, and in the very center of the metropolis rose an immense pile of masonry wrought in the likeness of a tremendous human figure, seated tailor-fashion. Its head bore seven faces, each of which looked in a different direction, and showed a different expression.

"That is the Archtemple," said the Illusionist, "the residence of the Holy Hierophant; you will notice that it has been fashioned into the likeness of Gulnazphaz, the premier divinity of the Horxite Pantheon, whose six other godlings are considered but facets or emanations of Gulnazphaz, and who are represented by the alternate faces on his head. The Archtemple is generally considered one of the Seventy Wonders of Gondwane, although I myself heartily dislike anthropomorphic architecture."

The Bazonga landed in the Heretics' Quarter, where outlanders, pagans, atheists, foreigners, and infidels resided; the other six quarters of the city were given over to subsidiary shrines, sacred colleges, monasteries and nunneries, and the residences of the innumerable priests, archpriests, underpriests, deacons, sextons, laity, pilgrims, oracles, and various ecclesiastic functionaries.

The quarter in which they sought a hostelry was not exactly a ghetto, Ganelon learned. That is, even the various pagans and infidels who therein resided were not really forbidden to enter the more sacrosanct precints of the city; but when they did leave the quarter, they were bound by law to display tabards on their person inscribed fore and aft with huge signs written in virulent pink on asparagus-green. These signs read:

BEWARE, O YE FAITHFUL!
THE WEARER BE AN ATROCIOUS IDOLATER
OF FALSE GODS AND INTERDICTED CULTS.
APPROACH HIM/HER/IT AT YOUR SOUL'S PERIL!

Ganelon heartily disliked being forced to wear the tabard, but as the Illusionist desired to consult one of the major Horxite oracles, whose shrine rose in a grove of sacred whuffwhuff trees in the Archdiocese of the Argaphraxian Fathers, he was forced to don the repulsive garment. To make matters worse, one of the ghetto guards insisted on walking eleven paces ahead of them, ringing a small bell and calling out "Unclean! Unclean!" at intervals.

Led by the ghetto guard, Ganelon and the Illusionist entered the Argaphraxian Quarter, feeling quite ridiculous in their tabards and given a wide berth by passersby, who generally crossed the street to avoid their proximity, and their taint of heresy.

"By the Purple Helix," the Illusionist fumed, "but this is inhospitable! To be forced to don these repulsive tabards is an affront; matters were not so when last I visited Holy Horx, I can assure you. A new exclusionist fervor has risen among the Horxites since the last Hierophantic election, I see! Were it not that I must consult the Argaphraxian Archives on the recent Elphodic Schism, I would happily forego this embarrassment."

For his part, Ganelon cared little if people avoided him; he gazed about with lively interest at the various shops, shrines, arcades, bazaars, suffumigatoriums, wayside chapels, marts, and manufactories.

In truth, the ecclesiastical center of the Horxite faith was a colorful and exotic city. Fortune-tellers, seers, prophets, theomancers, auric readers, and haruspices squatted on sidewalk mats beneath striped awnings. Dervish dancers spun dreamily beneath flowering belimia trees in the squares; itinerant exorcists and spell-erasers hawked their spiritual services from street corners and alley mouths. Booths and shops offered a variety of theological wares: holy water bottled under the Hierophantic seal, incense sticks, religious medals, periapts, talismans and amulets, portable folding shrines, copies of the Ninety Scriptures embossed on vellum, painted on silk, or inked on parchment scrolls, and books of a churchly nature.

The illusionist paused to scrutinize these last wares. They consisted entirely of the Scriptures, extracts of the Scriptures, digests of the Scriptures, and commentaries on the Scriptures; the book-merchant also sold volumes of collected sermons, Exemplary Lives, volumes of hagiography, and biographies of the Holy Hierophants of yore. No secular literature of any kind was proffered for sale, all such fluffery deemed irrelevant, if not actually irreverent, and banned by Hierophantic edict.

"What is it you hope to find in these Archives?" Silvermane asked. The Illusionist shrugged.

"The Airmasters are a religious offshoot of the Horxites," he said. "Thirty-two years ago, that old zealot, Vlydabec, was defeated in the ecclesiastical election. Rebuffed in his attempts to achieve the Hierophancy, he proclaimed himself the long-awaited Elphod of the Horxite faith—a sort of *mahdi*. The new Hierophant promptly excommunicated him; *he* promptly excommunicated the Hierophant and withdrew to Sky Island in a huff, surrounded by a few faithful followers. Very swiftly he gained spiritual authority over the Sky Islanders, and the present troubles began. The Archives retain the salient facts of his pre-schismatic career and some basic information concerning the dogmas and doctrines of the splinter sect which he founded. Ah, here we are, I believe!"

They entered a circular courtyard about which a coliseum-shaped building of considerable extent was built in the Hadhazy style of architecture. At the portal the Illusionist requested an interview with the Curator of Heretical Dossiers. In a few moments the attendant returned, saying the curator would see him in half an hour. Ganelon yawned and began to fidget.

"Listen, my boy, these matters will be of no interest to you, so why don't you stroll about and see the sights? Be careful not to enter any of the temples, for the Horxites would raise a terrible rumpus at that. The physical intrusion of an infidel, you see, would ineffably pollute the holy precincts."

"Very well, master."

"Don't get lost, now; try not to go out of sight of the Archives; and for Galendil's sake, try to stay out of trouble!"

"Yes, master."

The Illusionist entered the cool shadowy arcade to await his summons into the Praeceptorium. Silvermane strolled about the courtyard, then ambled out into the street, preceded by the ghetto guard and his warning bell.

The street led into a very large and crowded bazaar; Ganelon headed for it, not realizing the extraordinary sequence of events he was about to set into motion.

17.

THE "RESCUING" OF XARDA

The bazaar was certainly a huge one, by the standards of Zermish, at any rate, and was crowded with a throng numbering many hundreds. In almost no time at all Ganelon became separated from the ghetto guard; a few minutes later the wheels of a passing carriage narrowly missed him. They did not miss a thick puddle of noisome mud; in fact they raised a shower of stinking fluid that sluiced the unwary giant from head to foot. Grumbling disgustedly, Ganelon retired to the mouth of an alley, struggled out of his mud-soaked heretic's tabard and looked about for a way to cleanse away the filth. A nearby fountain caught his eye. Bundling the dripping garment under one arm he plowed through the throng and began rinsing out the reeking garment in the fresh running water.

Before he had quite completed this task, however, a woman's sharp, agonized cry reached his ears. She sounded as if she were in trouble: certainly she was in pain. Dropping the muddy tabard to the pavement, the giant craned about, searching for the source of the disturbance. Some distance away he perceived a line of chained men and women being escorted by green-robed priests. One of these unfortunates, a strong, handsome young girl clad in an abbreviated garment made up of bronze plates and scraps of chainmail, had fallen to the ground, having stumbled over some obstacle. One of the green-robed attendants had begun to methodically flog her on the back and shoulders with a length of whip. As Ganelon watched, the girl flushed with fury, reached out, caught the priest by his bony ankles, jerked his feet out from under him, and caused him to flop over, bashing his shaved skull against the paving stones.

A gasp of horror went up from the throng of marketgoers who had swiftly gathered to observe the girl's chastisement with avid eyes. Obviously, in Holy Horx, one simply did not yank a priest's feet out from under him.

"There, you scrawny lout—let's see how *you* like it now!" snapped the girl, scrambling to her feet. Snatching up the whip, she began laying stinging strokes across the bony shoulders of her former tormentor, who yelped and wriggled and cried for help.

Nine or ten others, similarly robed and baldpated, and armed with whips, prods, or cudgels, hurriedly bore down on the girl to rescue their upended brother. Undaunted, the girl spread her long, lithe, bare legs, and faced them with a scowl and a glare, the whip raised and ready for action, clenched in one small, firm, capable fist.

Nine or ten against one were unfair odds, thought Ganelon. He admired the boldness and spirit of the armored girl, and desired to learn why she was in chains. As the angry priests ringed her about he stepped forward and bade them desist. Outside of an astounded glance over their shoulders, they paid him no further attention. So he reached out, seizing two of them by the scruff of the neck, and pitched them head over heels into the fountain.

The crowd hastily backed away, averting their eyes from this impiety; but the remaining priests were too busy trying to beat the girl into insensibility to notice the fate of their hapless comrades. Growling a repetition of his former injunction that they desist, the bronze giant strode among them, clouting with balled fists to either side. In less time than it would take to describe it, five or six limp bodies lay tossed about, either knocked out cold, or whimpering through mouthfuls of broken teeth.

The girl had staggered and fallen under their beating; Ganelon helped her to her feet and inquired solicitously as to her injuries.

"Injuries? If you think those feeble-wristed runtlings could deal an injury to a knightrix of Jemmerdy, you are seriously mistaken!" the girl snorted, tossing back an unruly curl.

Her eyes widened as she got a good look at the towering young giant. For his own part, Ganelon was admiringly examining the lithe, sturdy girl. She was slim and bare-legged, her head scarcely reaching his mid-chest. She had sparkling green eyes, huge in her firm-chinned face, framed by tousled red hair. Freckles were attractively scattered across her sunburned cheeks and small snub-nose. With her scratched, bare knees, smudged face, and small, firm-breasted figure, she looked like an adolescent. Ganelon thought her quite the prettiest creature he had ever seen, save for the languorous and seductive river-nix, Alyx.

"By my halidom!" she marveled. Spying the Zermetic amulet his father Phlesco had hung around his neck at their last parting, she said, "A Zermishman, eh? Well, they certainly grow them big in Zermish!" Then she grinned impishly. "Thanks for coming to my aid, anyway—although it won't do us much good in the end." She nodded toward the senior of the priests Silvermane had laid out with his big fists. Groggily nursing a goose-egg lump on his bruised pate, the priest was tooting shrilly on a brass whistle slung around his skinny throat. From the far side of the market plaza a troop of twenty Civil Peace Monitors were converging on them, kite-shields lifted and spears leveled ominously.

"All I did was stop them from beating you," said Silvermane, puzzled. "What's wrong with that?" The girl eyed him solemnly, then grinned again in that frank, impish way he found so appealing.

"I'm a Lapsed Convert, condemned to the slave-block," she said. "That means I'm a foreigner visiting here from one of the territories claimed by the Hierophant to be Horxite. Actually, it's been a thousand years since the Kingdom of Jemmerdy declared its independence of Horxite rule, and we worship the way we please. But these holy ignoramuses have their own very selective views on ancient history; once a Horxite, always a Horxite to them!"

"But that's not fair!" Ganelon said, bewildered. "Surely these people can't just put you in chains and sell you into slavery because your remote ancestors used to be under the rule of their remote ancestors!"

"Oh, no? Tell that to the Hierophant! Or his soldiers, that is. Here they come!"

"Surrender, vile, priest-smiting Heretics!" bellowed a burly sergeant in a foghorn voice, as the troop came up to them. Ganelon stepped forward, spreading his empty hands in a mollifying gesture.

"You fellows don't understand—this girl is just a visitor from another country, arrested for no good reason—they were beating her, and I stopped them—"

Looking him over with narrowed eyes, the sergeant suddenly sucked in his breath between discolored teeth.

"An untabarded Heretic!" he gargled. "Take them, boys!"

A spear darted at Ganelon's unprotected stomach. The big man seized hold of it, shook the soldier off the other end, and broke it in half. Then, as the troopers bunched to charge him, he turned, took hold of a farmer's wooden wain standing nearby, heaved it up over his head with a surge of gigantic muscles that drew unbelieving gasps from the throng—and threw it at them!

They went down like tenpins, knocked sprawling by the heavy cart. Ganelon grabbed the girl's hand.

"Come on," he said.

They went pelting off toward the mouth of the nearest alley, timid citizens shrinking from their path in fright. Once the darkness of the alley had swallowed them up, Ganelon bent, broke the chains on the girl's wrists, tossed her over one shoulder, and took to his heels in earnest.

Ganelon *ran*. And when the Construct really exerted himself, there was hardly anything on two legs, or four, or even six, which had much chance of overtaking him.

"Where—*whumph!*—are we—*whuff!*—going?" gasped the girl knight from her undignified position.

"Back to the Heretics' Quarter," Ganelon said briefly. "My friend the Bazonga is there; she can carry you to safety by air."

Ganelon did not bother trying to explain what the Bazonga was; the girl would be finding out for herself soon, if luck was with them.

Which is was not. Evidently, the internal intelligence system maintained by the Civic Peace Monitors was an excellent and quite efficient one.

For, when they arrived before the gates of the wall-enclosed quarter, these were closed and barred. And half a hundred mounted bowmen of the ghetto guard sat their mounts before them, arrows nocked.

Ganelon let the girl down at her insistence. Together they inspected the opposition thoughtfully. Even Ganelon had to agree it was formidable.

"There's only fifty of them; that's not so bad. I bet I could fight them . . ." Ganelon let his words trail off under the girl's reproving eye.

"I believe you just might," she sighed. "But it's no use, you know. And the Sirix Xarda of Jemmerdy will not per-

mit an innocent friend to die in her defense; such is forbidden by the Chivalric code. Let us surrender, and throw
ourselves upon the mercy of the court."

"If any," Ganelon grumbled under his breath. But he
did as the Sirix wished.

One branch of the Ecclesiastic Tribunal stood in perpetual open session in a building just opposite the gate to the
Heretics' Quarter, since the troublesome pagans and infidels were almost continuously in breech of one or another
of the sacred Horxian laws. Ganelon and Xarda had a
trial which lasted all of four minutes.

"The male creature is guilty of Tabard Discarding, In-
terruption of Priestly Duties, Disturbance of the Civic
Tranquility, Ecclesiastical Assault, Defiance of the Peace
Monitors, Unwarranted Flight, Theft of Hierophantic
Property, Kidnapping of Hierophantic Property, and Exceeding the Speed Limit," droned a bored Justiciar. "The
female, already adjudged guilty of Lapsed Conversion, is
newly guilty of Resisting Chastisement, Ecclesiastical Assault, Defiance of the Peace Monitors, Unwarranted
Flight, Maintaining a Dangerous Confederate, and in aid-
ing and abetting each of the nine points of Unlawfulness
whereof her accomplice has just been adjudged guilty. The
case is closed; the culprits are to be sold into slavery for
the Public Good."

Within half an hour, Ganelon Silvermane and Xarda of
Jemmerdy were sold to the Tigermen, were condemned to
labor in the Air Mines of Karjixia, and departed for
Karjixia in a Tigermanic slave caravan.

18.

THE AIR MINES
OF KARJIXIA

The work was not as difficult as Ganelon had feared.
The frozen oxygen crumbled doughily before the bite
of the pickax and was a light, inconsequential burden

when shoveled into the go-carts. The mine slaves labored at shifts of twelve-hours-on and twelve-hours-off, which was grueling at first until one got used to it. With his towering height and bulging thews, it was only natural that the overseer would assign him to the Deep Pits. Smaller, slighter, and less strong, Xarda was assigned to light labor at the Sifting Bins, where the frozen powder was raked clean of impurities and bagged for shipment to the Dome Villages.

It was a friendly guard named Aarghax who explained to Ganelon what it was all about. The renegade Horxites who had taken refuge on Sky Island had converted and soon dominated the Quasihumans in residence there. The aerial island commonly floated to and fro over Karjixia and Quay, sometimes driven as far as Ixland during the Windy Season. As soon as the Elphod had got the upper hand, he began exacting tribute from the Quaylies and the Ixlanders through the simple expedient of threatening to drop Sky Islandish garbage upon their cities. As for Karjixia, he found an even more appropriate mode of exacting tribute: In the jungles of the Tigermen there existed the so-called Death Zone. This was an immense bubble of pure vacuum, trapped beneath the heavy, humid atmosphere of Karjixia and unable to escape.*

This bubble of space vacuum was believed to have been sucked down to the earth's surface a generation ago when the head of a comet collided with the mountains of central Karjixia. The Elphod, who had benefited from an excellent technological education at Vandalex in his youth, found a method by which the vacuum bubble could be extended to swallow nearby parcels of real estate. He then caused the Death Zone to absorb two villages of the Tigermen, asphyxiating the inhabitants on the spot; following this demonstration of his powers, he demanded tribute from other nearby villages, upon threat of moving the vacuum bubble to their localities.

The Tigermen fiercely resented this form of blackmail, and soon found means of rejecting the demands of the so-called Airmasters (as the Sky Islanders had taken to calling themselves). For the comet's head, a gigantic mass of

* Scientifically impossible, according to the present state of knowledge, of course. But remember: in seven hundred million years the Laws of Nature have undergone change and alteration.

frozen oxygen, nitrogen, hydrogen, and helium, was buried
beneath the roots of the Thazarian Mountains; mines were
soon sunk, and the frozen air thus brought to the surface
was used to supply breathable atmosphere to those towns
and villages which had been domed over against fluctua-
tions in the Death Zone.

Everything that came into the vacuum bubble was destroyed; every living thing, that is. Deprived of air, the
jungle vegetation withered and crumbled, and the denizens
of the tropic forests died. If the Airmasters maintained the
vacuum bubble over one particular area for seven days or
more, that region was transformed into a stretch of sterile
desert. As yet, only some fifteen or sixteen towns of the
Tigermen were immediately threatened; but the Elphod
was rumored to be tinkering with devices that would en-
able him to move the bubble at will over considerable dis-
tances—and even to extend its size.

For the time being, said Aarghax, the Air Mines were
sufficient to supply the Dome Villages with air. But the
deposit of cometary debris would not be enough to supply
more than twenty-three such communities, were so many
to be enveloped in the vacuum bubble. The Tigermen,
however, were impotent to strike back at the Airmasters,
since Sky Island was now maintained stationary at a
height of some three miles aloft.

It was a stalemate. But how long it would stay that way
was anybody's guess.

Aarghax was an average Tigerman and representative
of his peculiar race. The Tigermen were a new species of
Nonhumans which had come into being only during the
last fifty thousand years, evolving into bipedal form and
mental sentience from feline ancestors. They stood only
five feet tall, but were sinewy and sinuous, tenacious foes
and superb fighters. They resembled the human species
only vaguely, having prick-ears, sensitive whiskers, powerful fangs, yellow eyes with slit-pupils, and retractable
claws in hands and feet. Their rippling, steely muscled
bodies were lithe and lissome, and moved with feline
grace. From head to toe they were covered with a short
silken nap of tawny-yellow fur, barred with chocolate-
brown stripes, hence their name.

Neither Ganelon nor the girl had been ill-treated during
the caravan trek. The Tigermen were not cruel or

vicious, unlike certain of their domesticated ancestors. They were, in fact, a friendly and peaceable race, fond of dancing and jumping sports; their diet consisted principally of river fish. They went naked, their furry nap rendering garments unnecessary, and mated only twice a year. Human females were uninteresting to them; therefore they had offered no insult to the girl knight, much to Ganelon's relief.

The principal discomfort of air mining was the extreme cold. The oxygen and other gases in the head of the comet had been quick-frozen eons ago in the black spaces between the stars; so intensely frozen were the atmospheric gases that the blue snow mined from the roots of the Thazarian Mountains had to be cooked in charcoal furnaces before the life-giving vapors could be released into the roofed villages. Those hapless slaves whose task it was to dig up the frozen cometary vapors suffered exceedingly from the supra-arctic rigor that permeated the mines. Ganelon, stronger and hardier than the other slaves, suffered to a lesser degree.

He could not understand why the Illusionist had not come after them. During the ten-day trek from Horx to Karjixia, he had expected at any given moment to observe against the sky the ungainly form of the Bazonga bird. When this looked-for apparition failed to appear, he eventually concluded that the Illusionist, too, had been arrested by the Horxite fanatics.

Aarghax, who enjoyed chatting with those of the slave miners who were not reduced to mindless docility by their imprisonment, told Ganelon that the prince of the Tigermen, one Vrowl the Fifth, had recently been approached by an embassy of Sky Islanders who threatened to extend the vacuum bubble over the entirety of Karjixia. Prince Vrowl swore he would not rest until every town and village in the kingdom was domed against the vacuum; to this the Sky Islanders smilingly agreed, saying they would thereupon sell air to the dome-dwellers at a fixed rate, since soon the atmosphere over Karjixia would be entirely under their control. The prince of the Tigermen had commanded the ambassadors be returned to the safety of Sky Island before he personally scratched their eyes out.

Upon receiving this news, Ganelon more than ever wished his master were here. For the Illusionist professed great friendliness toward the poor Tigermen, and would have resented and opposed this attempt at an air monopoly with every means at his disposal.

In the absence of the Illusionist, however, it seemed to Ganelon that it was up to him to help the Tigermen.

"That's awfully dumb," said Xarda one evening as they shared a bowl of fish-stew. "Why do you want to help these creatures? They have chained us and work us like dogs! I would enjoy nothing more than escaping from here in such a manner that I left a few dozen striped and prick-eared corpses behind me. For a Sirix of the Chivalry of Jemmerdy to toil like a grubby field laborer under the eyes of a bunch of overgrown cats is an insult I shall not forget!"

"I don't know," Silvermane said doggedly. "If my master were here, he would want me to help the poor Tigermen. Even though he isn't here, I know it's what he would want me to do."

"In that case, you can count me out," the girl knight declared firmly. "I'll help in any way if you intend trying to escape from here, but I'll not lend my sword to the aid of our oppressors!"

"Very well, then, I'll have to try it alone," said Ganelon.

Ganelon was curious as to how the Airmasters traveled between their aerial floating kingdom and the surface of Gondwane. Here again the friendly Tigerman was able to give him the information he required.

"They have domesticated the Phlygûl and ride about in wooden saddles strapped across their shoulders," said Aarghax.

"Indeed? And what are the Phlygûl?" asked Silvermane.

"Monstrous creatures eleven feet tall equipped with glaring eyes, hollow blood-sucking fangs, and batwings with a thirty-foot wingspread," said the Tigerman. "These quasihumans were the original inhabitants of Sky Island, quickly subjugated by the Horxite schismatics."

"Really? I don't believe I have ever heard of such creatures."

"Maybe not, but if you are ever unlucky enough to see a Phlygûl, you'll know what it is," replied the Tigerman, shivering slightly.

19.

THE DEATH ZONE MOVES SOUTH

The very next day messengers came galloping on lathered orniths, bearing messages of great import to the garrison leader in charge of the Air Mines. The messengers had ridden all morning, having departed from Xombol, the capital of the Tigermen's kingdom, at the first break of day.

"I wonder what's up," mused Silvermane. The other slaves shrugged indifferently; little that could possibly happen to interrupt their apathy was of interest to them.

Aarghax strolled over, his long striped tail lashing nervously. Ganelon asked him what had occurred.

"The vacuum bubble is on the move again," the Tigerman hissed, glaring at the distant black mote far above, which was Sky Island. "They say it's moving south."

"Aren't these Air Mines directly south of the Death Zone area?"

"Hmm. Yes—more or less. Don't worry about it; the Airmasters probably intend to envelop Doraad with the Zone," he said, mentioning a small, as-yet-undomed village directly north of the mountains. "The mayor of Doraad has most recently defied the demands of the Airmasters. Nothing to do with us here, I'm sure. Back to work, you lazy humans! Move along, now."

"I wonder," Silvermane mused to himself. "It would not be unintelligent of the Sky Islanders to extend the Death Zone over the mining area; that would asphyxiate the guards and miners, and would effectively cut off air shipments to the Dome Villages."

"It would also kill *us*," snapped the girl knight, vexed. "Or doesn't that concern you? I swear, boy, you are more worried about your purring furry friends than you are about your fellow humans!"

Silvermane sighed, but made no rebuttal. How could he

101

explain to the soldierly girl that, as a Construct, he was as close to the Tigermen—or even to the monstrous, bat-winged Phlygûl—as he was to True Men?

Silvermane was on the second shift, which began its work at noon. Hence he was still above the surface, strapping into his insulated garments for work in the frigid depths of the Air Mines, when the Death Zone struck.

The first inkling any of them had of the approaching vacuum wall was when the cook-fires began winking out. These small bonfires had been burning furiously beneath iron caldrons of simmering stew, just prepared for the midday meal. Then, one by one, the fires were snuffed out as if by an invisible giant's hand. Yaargha, the burly-chested Tigerman cook, was the first living being struck down. He suddenly dropped the huge iron spoon with which he had been stirring the stew-pot; it bounced off the flat stones that ringed the firepit, but—very strangely—they heard no *clang* when the iron implement clattered against the stones.

"That's odd," Ganelon murmured to Xarda. The girl was about to ask him what he was talking about, when the peculiar actions of Yaargha caught her bright green gaze. The Tigerman staggered, clutching at his heavy throat; his yellow eyes bulged almost from their sockets; his fanged and bewhiskered jaws gaped open in the most alarming manner; then hot blood gushed from his distended nostrils and he fell to the ground, writhing as if being swiftly strangled by some unknown assailant.

Ganelon seized the girl knight's arm as the fire Yaargha had been tending suddenly went out—completely out; even the glowing coals blackened and died instantly.

"Let go of me, you big lummox!" the girl said, wriggling in his grasp. "Yaargha's sick—"

"Yaargha is dead," growled Silvermane, hackles bristling. "*The Death Zone is upon us.*"

Then, without any further remonstrations or waste of words, the bronze giant scooped up the girl in his arms and headed for the edge of the jungle. The Sirix of Jemmerdy was like a child in the grasp of his mighty arms; her head pillowed against the dark, massively muscled shield of his chest, the girl permitted herself to be borne away without further protest. Suddenly she had realized the significance of what she had seen: the iron spoon had made no sound when it fell against the stones, because sounds could not travel through a vacuum.

It was as Silvermane had morosely predicted: it would be shrewd and foresighted of the Airmasters to devastate and depopulate the mining regions, thus depriving even the Dome Villages of the life-supporting supplies of precious vapor!

Silvermane entered the borders of the jungle, moving at the speed of an express train. The sudden and unexpected advance of the dreaded vacuum bubble had thrown the administration of the camp into complete disorder. Thus no guards sought to interfere with the giant as he bore the girl off in his arms, and they were able to make their escape without even the necessity of breaking a few heads.

The raw jungle vegetation had been crudely hacked down around the entrance to the mines, creating a raw clearing of stamped earth about two hundred square yards in extent. To one side stood the barracks of the laborers, enclosed in a palisade fence topped with spikes and patrolled by Tigermen guards. The guards themselves, about one hundred warriors strong, lived in huts scattered about the perimeter of the clearing. Beyond the circle of guard-huts, a barrier of packed earth rose to the height of some ten feet or so, partially to discourage entry into the camp by jungle predators, and partly to discourage escape from the camp by any of the laborers. Ganelon cleared the top of the earthworks with a single gigantic leap.

He forged a path into the jungle for about half a mile before he came to a halt and set the breathless girl upon her feet again. The giant stood listening, an expression of intense concentration visible upon his features.

"Whatever are you listening for?" the girl knight demanded sharply. It rather offended her sense of knightly self-sufficiency to be rescued by a man; and, besides, she was heartily annoyed that Ganelon had been astute enough to detect the approach of the Death Zone before she did. "Do you think you'll be able to hear the vacuum coming?" she inquired sarcastically.

He nodded somberly. "Vegetation crushes in upon itself when in the vacuum," he said. "We should be able to hear the crunching of collapsing wood and brush. . . ."

But no such sounds were audible; after a time, the giant relaxed. As far as he could tell, the Death Zone had been extended only to cover the mining camp and the entrances to the shafts; it did not seem to be encroaching upon the jungle at all.

They discussed this in low tones; Ganelon wanted to return through the jungle to see if any of the slaves and guards still lived. Xarda, on the other hand, argued that doubtless all were slain and that they should continue making their escape while they could, putting as much distance between them and the vacuum-smothered slave camp while they were able to do so. Her rational arguments won the day over the humane impulses of the tenderhearted Construct. They pushed on. It was less than an hour past midday; they had all afternoon to travel, and during that expanse of time doubtless they could find a secure refuge in which to spend the night. It made better sense to travel by day than by night, since during the hours of darkness the monsters of the jungle woke and hunted.

As they strolled along together side by side, the girl a diminutive, childlike figure beside the brawny giant, she stole an occasional thoughtful look at him with a sidewise flick of her green eyes.

The kingdom of Jemmerdy was not a woman-dominated realm run by Amazons, such as the country of the Warrior Women of Khond. Hereditary kings ruled in Vladium, the Jemmerdine capital, and males gnerally held the chief administrative posts. But the men of Jemmerdy were given to intellectual and artistic pursuits, with little or no interest in, or proclivity for, the arts of war. Hence it had always been the custom in Jemmerdy for young women between the ages of fourteen and (if unmarried) forty, to hold positions in the Nine Knightly Fellowships which comprised the army of the Jemmerdines. At seventeen, Xarda was dubbed knight—or "knightrix," as the female soldiers were called in her homeland. She was not exactly contemptuous of men, but never before had she met a male who was bolder, stronger, swifter, or more valiant than she. Never until meeting Ganelon Silvermane, that is.

She peered curiously into the impassive bronze mask of his face, wondering what he was thinking about. The young giant excited her, impressed her, annoyed her, and in a way frightened her a little. One of the things which annoyed her most, although she was not aware of it, was that the gigantic youth seemed totally unaware of the fact that she was extremely attractive, more than half naked, and just a bit susceptible to his masculinity.

"What are you thinking about, with that grim look on your face?" she asked after a steady hour of progress through the humid jungle.

"Sky Island," he said, nodding toward the sky, patches of which were visible through rents in the foliage over their heads. The aerial kingdom hung, a tiny black mote against the hot blue afternoon sky, to the north. "We're free now, and part of my plan to help the Tigermen is accomplished. But how can I get to that height? The Airmasters fly between heaven and earth astride their Phlygûl, but I have no Phlygûl." In response to her next query he painted a word-picture of the hideous, batwinged flying monsters with the thirty-foot wingspread about which Aarghax had told him.

The monsters sounded indescribably frightful. Falling silent, Xarda could not get them out of her mind. Thus, a few moments later, when an enormous shadow fell over them and she looked up to see a fearful winged monster descending upon them, and she screamed deafeningly, the only thing that entered her stunned and frozen mind was—the Phlygûl were coming for them!

20.

A PEACE CRISIS IN JEMMERDY

The immense winged shape floated down to the jungle floor and bent upon the two a severe eye.

"My goodness, child! There's no need to *shriek* so; I swear you have cracked my tympana. And as for my nerves—!"

The girl knight shrank into the cirle of Silvermane's arms.

"What is that dreadful thing?" she whispered.

"It's a Bazonga," Ganelon said happily.

"*The* Bazonga, I'll have you know! The only one there is; and prominently featured in a popular creed, I am told," the bird-vessel corrected him in scandalized tones. " '*A* Bazonga,' indeed!"

"Dear bird, where is my master?" Ganelon inquired anxiously.

"I'm here, you great idiot," snapped a peevish voice from the floor of the cockpit. A robed shape struggled into view. "This cursed contraption spied your auric emanations from the air and descended with such abruptness, I lost my footing," grumbled the magician, setting his disarranged garments straight with a jerk of his gloved hands. Then he studied Ganelon with a gaze whose fierceness could not disguise its affection.

"You seem to be all in one piece, at least. I hope this will teach you a lesson, my boy! 'Try to stay out of trouble,' I said; so of course you immediately tried to take on half the priests in Horx single-handed, to say nothing of two-thirds of the civic law-enforcers, get hauled up before an ecclesiastical court, and sold into slavery in a foreign realm—all within the space of two hours!"

The giant put his hands behind his back and hung his head as if unwilling to meet his master's eye, like a small boy being reprimanded for stealing cookies.

"Yes, master. I'm sorry, master, truly I am. But it's not my fault, really! They were beating this girl with whips, and they wouldn't stop when I told them to. So what else could I do?"

The Illusionist examined the still-frightened girl curiously. Then his manner softened, and he chuckled.

"Chivalry is still alive and well in Northern YamaYamaLand, I preceive! Well, my boy, this once I will forgive you for disobeying my instructions. And now perhaps you should introduce me to this young lady. . . ."

Before Ganelon could introduce them, the girl spoke up in a brisk, defiant voice. He got the impression she was heartily annoyed with herself for having displayed fear when the monstrous bronze bird had descended upon them.

"Hail, sorceror! I am the Sirix Xarda of Jemmerdy; knightrix first-class-with-bannerol in the Ancient and Noble Order of the Oliphaunt and Star."

The Illusionist permitted no trace of his amusement to

appear in his voice as he returned the greeting and introduced himself.

"I have heard of the lady knights of Jemmerdy," he mused. "Are you not rather far from your kingdom, young lady? On a quest, perhaps? I believe such is still the custom in your quaint and charming homeland, which I have not visited, I regret to say, for the better part of half a century. . . ."

Xarda relaxed her knightly stance to the extent of giving him a wary smile. "Not exactly a quest, Magister; I was engaged in searching for employment as a mercenary swordswoman when those repulsive Horxite bullies arrested me on the most absurd and unreasonable charges imaginable. Jemmerdy, you see, has fallen into a Peace Crisis; our present monarch, Maresco the Seventh, is given to scholarly and learned pursuits, to an even greater degree than are most of the Jemmerdine males. In order to enjoy his bibliophiliac studies in a mood of unbroken tranquility, quite early in his reign, the king concluded peace concordats with all realms, kingdoms, duchies, and baronies adjacent to our borders; and none of our neighbors has, as yet, seen fit to break a single one of them!"

"A distressing occurrence." The Illusionist smiled. "Or, more precisely, lack of occurrence! Pray continue, my dear."

"We of the Nine Knightly Orders were thus left with little or nothing to do except to maintain the internal security of our nation," the girl explained. "This was remarkably easy to do, since, as you probably know, the men of Jemmerdy are, virtually without exception, ridiculously peaceful, law-abiding, and artistic or scholarly. And most of the girls and women of the realm, who would normally be given to feuds, vendettas, duels, or other typically feminine interests, were already enrolled in one or another of the Knighthoods, since the recent recruitment drives have proved miraculously efficient. Knighthood, you understand, promises a colorful and exciting life of action, adventure, and derring-do, such as every red-blooded woman normally craves."

"A wave of peace hysteria doubtless swept the citizenry, then," said the Illusionist, amused.

The girl knight nodded grimly, red curls bobbing.

"It was simply terrible! Simple nothing to do. After all, a healthy womanly thirst for violence and bloodshed can only for a certain length of time be sated by tournaments, field maneuvers, weapons. practice, war games, and other such tame endeavors. I decided I had a bellyful of peace-time pap, and set out to procure martial employment in foreign lands less cursed by threats of unbroken tranquility than my own. I came here, you might say, on an extended leave of absence from my Order."

"I heartily sympathize with your unfortunate predic-ament, my. dear! Ganelon, I commend you on your choice of a damsel worthy of rescue; just this once I will say I approve of your impulse to transgress my edicts and admit you were quite right in following the instincts of your heart. Well, I must say, you led us a merry chase, though!"

"I was afraid they had arrested you, too, master," said the young giant.

"Oh, they did, they did, my boy! I believe the counts against me included such novel charges as Fomenting Dis-sension, Conspiracy to Transgress the Peace, and Nurtur-ing Blasphemy in, however, only the Second Degree. How-ever, it is not for nothing that I have spent the equivalent of more than a few ordinary human life-spans in the mas-tery of the magical arts and sciences. As soon as those self-righteous idiots had clapped me. in the city jail I con-cocted a few mind apparitions resembling the frightful In-digons who had, so very recently, harried the Horxite borders on their way south to the mountains. I believe the total of my illusory Indigons ran to an estimated *seventy* thousand; more than enough to plunge the excitable priest-lings into a holy frenzy, I assure you! As soon as the dom-inant hierarchy had locked themselves in that immense an-thropomorphic temple of theirs, the one which resembles a red-brick colossus squatting at stool—"

"Yes, master, I remember it well. You said they called it 'the Archtemple. . . .' "

"Quite right. Well, as soon as they were all locked away behind those fortresslike walls, which they presumed would protect them against what they fancied was an im-minent invasion of those blue monsters you so effectively scattered at the Battle of Uth, I called the Bazonga to me by a mental command issued on the wavelength employed by sentient crystalloids such as herself. You recall, we had parked the creature on the roof of our hostelry, tethering her to a chimney. . . . Well, with such alacrity did the dear

Bazonga respond to my mental summons that she not only reduced the chimney of the unfortunate hostelry to a mound of rubble, but burst the walls of the jailhouse asunder in her concern to free me from confinement."

The Illusionist regarded the great creature with fondness. "I begin to perceive the inestimable value of possessing a vehicle that is a friend as well as a mode of transport!" Then, turning to the mystified girl knight, he explained: "The Bazonga is composed of solid bronze, you see, lightly dusted with yxium, which renders her thoroughly weightless. However negative her weight may be, the dear bird still possesses the enormous mass of her solid metallic construction, and, if you can imagine a flying, seven-ton battering ram of solid bronze, hurtling herself like a maddened bull against the flimsy brickwork of the jailhouse wall ... well, you can perhaps picture for yourself the sudden and dramatic method by which the kindly creature procured my freedom for me ...!"

"I can indeed," the girl murmured, her green eyes sparkling. Doubtless she was envisioning the immense usefulness such a weapon as the sentient vehicle would be when next the Knightly Orders of Jemmerdy enjoyed the pleasures of laying siege to castle, fortress, or recalcitrant city.

The Sirix Xarda began to realize with inner excitement and delight that a few trouble-prone adventurers such as Ganelon Silvermane and the Illusionist of Nerelon were just what the unfortunate kingdom of Jemmerdy needed in the current Peace Crisis.

21.

THE AIRMASTERS' ULTIMATUM

The Bazonga bird's cockpit held seats enough for six passengers, so there was more than enough room within the voluble vehicle for the Illusionist, Silvermane, and the girl knight from Jemmerdy.

"Where to, master?" the bird-creature chirped brightly.

The Illusionist briefly consulted his chart and delivered directions for Xombol, the capital of the country of the Tigermen. This was the nearest large city, and, as the Illusionist was definitely *persona plus grata* with the ruler of the Tigermen, he envisioned no particular difficulties in passing off the two escaped Air Miners as his wards or pupils.

Ganelon and Xarda still wore their slave garments; these consisted of kiltlike short skirts about the loins, dyed the shrieking scarlet of slavery. Above the waist they wore nothing. This semi-nudity did not bother the girl, accustomed as she was to the rough, hardy life of barracks, camp, and field: neither did it bother the simple young giant, who had not as yet displayed any emotional awareness of the opposite sex.

It did, however, offend the sensibilities of the Illusionist. A confirmed bachelor, the master-magician of Nerelon found the small, adolescent breasts of Xarda a distraction. Luckily, the luggage compartment built in the tail-section of the Bazonga still held Ganelon's duffel and gear, so the Construct simply tossed aside slavery's scarlet and donned his usual togs. The Illusionist found a spare robe of his own wherewith to clothe the half-naked girl.

They arrived in the city of Xombol in late afternoon, and found it in an uproar. Securing overnight quarters at a local inn, they inquired as to the occasion of the excited, snarling crowds that surged to and fro in the streets brandishing placards and smashing all objects in sight. The innkeeper, a corpulent Tigerman with one badly chewed ear (the token, he wheezed, of a slight domestic quarrel with his late wife), told them that word of the vacuumization of the Air Mines had reached the capital only shortly before, on the heels of a new ultimatum from the Airmasters of Sky Island.

"Indeed?" the Illusionist inquired coolly. "And what do the Sky Islanders demand this time by way of tribute?"

Growling under his breath, the fat innkeeper named a sum so prodigious as to represent the total graft accumulated by any average municipal officer over a lifetime of corruption.

"What brazen effrontery!" murmured the Illusionist. "Ganelon, my boy, store our gear in the room and rejoin Xarda and I as soon as you can. We shall be in the taproom."

"My son Grf will show you to your room, sir," puffed the fat innkeeper, pocketing the night's payment in advance. Silvermane hoisted their bags to one broad shoulder and followed the small waddling Tigercub to the third floor back, where he stowed their gear under the bed. He soon rejoined the Illusionist and the girl, who were refreshing themselves with huge wooden cups of strong brown ale.

"The first item on our agenda is to secure an appointment with the prince of the Tigermen, whose name is Vrowl the Fifth; I was on rather good terms with his late father, Vrowl the Fourth, so there should be no difficulty in obtaining—"

"Wrong," said Xarda. "The *first* item on our agenda is to purchase a few articles of feminine apparel! You go to the palace and interview the king of the cats, if you like; Ganelon and I will go shopping."

"Shopping!" protested the giant. "What do I know about ladies' clothing? I would be of no use to you in choosing such flummery! Besides, I want to go to the palace and see the prince of the Tigermen with my master."

"You," said Xarda with great finality, "will come with me and carry my bundles." And that was that.

As it was the end of the week, most of the shops in Xombol would not close until the ninth hour. Inquiring directions from the keeper's daughter, a languid, frowsy feline called Purrline, Xarda strode off down the street with Ganelon at her heels.

The Falling Moon had not yet arisen; strings of globular paper lanterns were strung across the lanes at intervals between tall poles obviously erected for that purpose. They glowed ice-blue, dusky-red, virulent-green, and canary-yellow through the purple dusk. Carriages clattered through the cobbled streets; resembling rickshaws, they were drawn by Tigermen coolies. Scorning the use of wheels, Xarda preferred to employ her own long legs. She strode along zestfully, glancing with bright, curious eyes to every side. They passed outdoor cafés where Tiger couples caroused about rickety tables; barber emporiums where whirring, motor-driven shaving machines cropped the tawny fur of Tigermen to fashionable lengths.

The frenzied crowds had surged off to drone and yowl

ominously in front of Prince Vrowl's palace, leaving the streets to ordinary citizens and visitors like themselves.

"I do hope Master doesn't get into any fuss with those protesters on his way to the palace," Ganelon said anxiously.

"Master," the girl said briskly, "can take care of himself. Come along now! we haven't all night."

The Street of the Armorers stood along the south bank of the Great Xombol Canal which conducted water through the city from an aqueduct to the north of Xombol; the aqueduct was connected with an estuary of Lake Romode.

Ganelon was relieved they were not to shop for ladies' hats or ribbons or undergarments. He followed Xarda admiringly as she briskly examined gorgets and greaves, haggled with armorers over the purity of their alloys, bringing down the price for every dent, seam, or loose bolt her keen eye spotted in the various articles of knightly apparel.

"You certainly know how to shop!" he said as he followed her out of one shop, his big arms laden with articles of chainmail and plate armor.

"My mother raised me to be a proper Jemmerdine woman," the girl explained. Shopping exhilarated her; she clinked the coins left in the purse the Illusionist had handed her before they parted. "Come along now. I must see to a decent cuirass and a longsword, if a fair bit of workmanship is to be found in this backwater. Don't drop that morion, you great lumbering oaf: if you dent it, I'll put a dent in you!"

They returned to the inn before moonrise, to find the Illusionist there before them. Xarda watched with a critical eye as Ganelon carefully bore her parcels to their room, then turned to the old magician with curiosity.

"I trust you got in to see Prince Vrowl?" she inquired.

He nodded. "Of course; no difficulty in that department whatever! The prince was delighted to see me, although in a vile temper over the insolence of the Airmasters in making this latest ultimatum of theirs. The Sky Islanders have the incredible gall to threaten the security of Xombol itself, unless the Tigermen beggar their royal treasury to buy them off."

"Zounds!" the girl knight exclaimed. "Such impertinence! I trust the Tigermen intend to unsheathe their claws and fight like women?"

The Illusionist shook his head.

"No chance of that, my dear, although they would love nothing more! But with the Air Mines incommunicado under the Death Zone, Prince Vrowl is helpless to oppose the Sky Islanders. As soon as the air supplies in the Dome Villages run low, Karjixia is helpless and at the mercy of the Airmasters."

"By my halidom!" Xarda swore. "Do you mean these great striped bullies mean to give in like a bunch of pussy-cats?"

"The Dome Villages have air supplies sufficient to last them another two days—three, if heavy exertion is banned and the shallow breathing regulations are enforced with rigor. Then they will have no recourse but to meet the demands of the Sky Islanders. And as for Xombol, doming it over is simply out of the question, due to its size. If the Airmasters fulfill their threat to move the Death Zone this far east, Prince Vrowl will have to pay the price or watch his suburbs asphyxiated, one by one."

The girl knight bridled with righteous indignation. Her innate sense of knightly fair play was outraged by the one-sidedness of it all.

"By the Gods, something must be done to help these people," she blazed. "I like them little, having slaved in their mines, but, after all, they are people! I am a knightrix, sworn to lend my blade to the defense of the defenseless, and sworn to strike a blow for justice against injustice! Is there nothing we can do to help the Tigermen?"

"There may be. I learned a few things from my researches back in Horx. The peculiar tenets of their sect contain some interesting contradictions which just might be exploited to their embarrassment and detriment."

"Well, what are we waiting for? That bird-ship of yours is parked on the roof—I have the armor I needed, and a decent sword again—Ganelon again has his war-gear and that odd, huge Silver Sword—what are we waiting for?"

The Illusionist stifled a yawn.

"My dear, impulsive child," he said. "'For ten days and nights I have been flying over mountains, deserts, and jungles, cooped up in a cold, drafty, uncomfortable cockpit, searching for the whereabouts of Ganelon Silvermane. In all that time I have not slept in a civilized bed, toasted my old shanks before a civilized fire, or filled my poor middle with a hot, civilized meal! Before we hurl our proverbial gauntlet in the very teeth of the Sky Islanders, I fully intend to enjoy all three of the abovementioned pleasures of civilization, for one night, at least."

"But—"

"But nothing, child. Sit down and look at this menu and wait for Ganelon to join us. This filet of river-monster in jingleberry sauce looks promising; perhaps a chef's salad on the side, swimming in Kakkawakka dressing; broiled tree-dwelling lobster with zik-butter; and a nicely chilled bottle of ciderfruit wine. Oh, my, yes!"

Xarda bit her lip and tried to restrain her knightly impatience, while the Illusionist sat back and prepared to enjoy with the gusto and finesse of a gourmet one of the civilized amenities he had been sorely missing of late.

Book Four

SILVERMANE ON SKY ISLAND

The Scene: The Jungles of Sky Island; the City of the Airmasters; the Death Machine.

Characters: Soldiers, Courtiers, Priests, Phlygûl, Airmasters; the First Holy Elphod; Jebd the Sky Serpent.

22.

MEETING WITH
A PHLYGÛL

Dawn rose in the east, flooding the vast supercontinent with light. No longer was the sun so brilliant as it had been in former Eons, the Illusionist reflected sleepily, as he washed his face and adjusted the lavender vapor before his features. Formerly it had burned a fierce, intolerable white; now a distinctly gold-yellow tinge dimmed its supernal fires. Summers were cooler than they had been even so recently as a million years before; and they would grow even cooler in the future as the Sun continued to age and dim its fires.

In a few million years, perhaps, the Sun would redden and begin to die, flickering like a candle blown in the wind, he knew. Unless the theorists of Vandalex were right after all, and the Sun was doomed to expand into a Red Giant at some future date. If that happened, all life on Old Earth would quickly perish as the oceans boiled away and the planet crumbled into a globe of molten rock.

Fretfully, the Illusionist turned his thoughts from doom and gloom. What did it matter, after all, how life would end? It would end in one way or another; all things which had beginnings also had endings. And, whether Old Earth froze or melted, an ending was an ending and one way was as good as another. He would not be here to learn how the story of man ended; he would be long gone, his place taken by another. He would cross over the brink of the Unknown, to explore the greatest mystery of all—the Mystery of Death.

Still, it would be nice to have all the answers, he thought. Then he grinned wryly behind his vapor-veil: even the Gods did not have all the answers, as he well knew, so why should he bemoan his own lack of omniscience,

Ganelon came clumping in to announce they were all packed and ready for the flight to Sky Island, and that Xarda was ordering breakfast.

"Be right with you, my boy. Just tidying up a bit; we must look our best when we confront the Holy Elphod, you know. Helps if you create a good impression sometimes!"

What with one thing and another, the Sun was well up by the time they were ready to climb into the cockpit of the Bazonga. It was, in fact, midmorning, but the Illusionist had lingered over his breakfast, his theory being that when one has much to do it is best to start the day off right. With a hearty meal under your belt, one is ready to wrestle monsters before lunch, was his way of putting it.

Xarda had slept on a pallet in the corner, chivalrously letting the old man enjoy the only bed and fastidiously declining to share it with him and Ganelon. As for the giant, he insisted on sleeping on the floor. Rolled up in blankets, he had stretched out before the door. His inexhaustible vigor obviously thrived on hardship; at any rate, the uncomfortable sleeping-place he had chosen had not impaired his slumbers, for his lusty snorings had kept the girl awake half the night. A hearty breakfast, however, put them all in a good mood, and they looked forward with zest toward their confrontation with the Airmasters.

As for their odd vehicle, she had spent the night drifting to and fro on the breeze, singing strange little songs, watching the stars wheel by overhead. The metal bird was pleased to see them and inquired perkily as to their plans for the day.

The Illusionist called her attention to the island in the sky, a dim mote some miles to the west. The floating isle looked to be at an altitude of about three miles; the Bazonga affably assured them that the power of her magnetic waves was more than sufficient to achieve such a height. Once they were all aboard and Ganelon had cast off the mooring line, the bird squawked out her zestful *tally-ho!* and they were aloft.

While the rooftops of the city of the Tigermen fell away beneath them, Xarda peered ahead with great curiosity at the aerial island. She had heard of such oddities, for four or five similar flying islands were known to savants, but as none of them happened to be located in the regions about Jemmerdy, she had never actually seen one before.

The Illusionist, who was never happier than when he had a chance to explain something to somebody, expanded graciously on the theme.

"No one really knows what holds such parcels of aerial real estate aloft," he said, "but the commonly accepted theory is simply that the Laws of Nature have reversed themselves in certain portions of Godwane; it is widely known that for the past hundred million years or more the natural laws have been passing through a state of flux, reversal, and alteration. Doubtless at one time the several flying islands were simply portions of the landscape, held to the surface of the supercontinent by the same gravitational forces which confine us all. Then, for some fairly inexplicable reason, in a few places gravity was suddenly reversed; vast chunks of soil and rock were sent hurtling into the sky. Some of them may have escaped from the embrace of the planet entirely, flying off into space to become asteroids or comet-heads; but four or five were trapped within Old Earth's atmosphere when the gravitational field reversed itself again."

"Yes, I understand that, Magister," the Sirix said politely. "But what I do not understand is why, when that happened, they did not simply come crashing down to Old Earth again."

"Well, no one really knows why that did not happen," the Illusionist confessed. "But perhaps the islands themselves are still under the effects of the reversed gravity field and are thus of negative weight; when the gravity pull of the land surface beneath them resumed its ordinary force, their negative weight was precisely balanced by their positive weight; this would make them as weightless as clouds—slightly more so, I imagine. At any rate, the Sky Islands are perfectly stationary aloft and will probably never come down again. Of course, no one can be positive about that, and most people with any sense have wisely refrained from making their homes directly under the floating islands, just in case."

"Well, it's certainly strange, you must admit," Xarda said pensively.

"Quite so; but, then, the world is filled with strange things here in the Last Days, in the Twilight of Time.

Many folk would doubtless say that a lady knight is a strange thing, or an intelligent metal bird that flies—"

"Or a talkative old geezer who covers his face with lavender smoke," the Bazonga bird cackled tartly.

"*Ahem!* There is no reason to venture into personalities, my dear bird: I was merely discoursing philosophically—"

"Philosophy is all very well," said the Bazonga bird. "For philosophers! But we are adventurers, bound on a quest of derring-do and all that sort of thing. Less chitchat and more action, say I!"

Ganelon cleared his throat. "Master."

"Just a moment, my boy, this talkative bird and I are—"

" 'Talkative bird' —indeed!" clacked the curious vehicle. "Talkative magician is more like it!"

"Master."

"Is that so?" the Illusionist snapped. "Well, let me tell you a thing or two. Bazonga! It has become perfectly obvious to me that my late esteemed colleague, Miomivir Chastovix, when selecting a sentient crystalloid to serve as the brain of his ungainly vehicle, chose one which is disrespectful, argumentative—"

"Please, master!"

"—impertinent, even snippy—"

"*Master!*" boomed Ganelon in a voice that made them all jump.

"Very well, what is it? These cursed interruptions!" snapped the Illusionist, fuming.

"We are about to meet one of those Phlygûl the Tigermen told me about," Silvermane stated solemnly.

"Eh?"

Ganelon pointed off to their left. Craning about, the others followed the direction of his hand and saw to their surprise and consternation a monstrous black-winged shape hurtling toward them through the skies.

"Oh, my goodness," the magician said breathlessly. "You're right—a thousand pardons for my inattention, my dear boy! That is certainly a Phlygûl, all right. . . ."

The thing's elongated body and gaunt, attenuated limbs were of a slick, glistening, rubbery black. It had immense cup-shaped ears and huge, glaring eyes that were red as glowing coals, and a wide, lipless mouth that fairly bristled with innumerable needle-teeth, startlingly white against its generally ebon coloration.

Its wings were ribbed and membranous and very closely resembled those of a bat—a bat with a thirty-foot wingspread. From its bony rear a long, muscular tail trailed away, terminating in a fanlike blade like a fishtail; it was by this means that the unearthly creature steered itself.

As it drew closer they could make out even more repulsive features of its anatomy. It had no nose, for example, and the lack of this familiar facial feature lent its visage an *unfinished* look that the travelers found singularly unsettling. It also lacked nipples and navel, which shed considerable doubt on the question of its mammalian antecedents. However, it did possess the organs of gender, which were repulsively huge and unquestionably male.

Uttering a shrill, squeaking cry that set their teeth on edge, the Phlygûl hurtled upon them. Ganelon sprang to his feet, brandishing the Silver Sword as the batwinged creature came at them. But the simple giant had evidently forgotten that he was in a flying machine, for as he jumped up the sudden motion and the shifting of his weight caused the bird-vehicle to sway sickeningly to one side.

Then Xarda screamed!

And Ganelon fell overboard.

23.

THE ISLAND ABOVE THE EARTH

To the Phlygûl, it must have looked as if the bronze giant with the glittering silvery mane deliberately sprang into the empty air to do battle with it. At any rate, startled by the sudden and unexpected leap, the Phlygûl veered off at the last moment. Its wings of tough membrane boomed like the sails of a frigate as they caught the rushing wind. Xarda and the Illusionist caught a brief, sickening gust of noisome reek from its body odor as it narrowly avoided collision with the vehicle. It stank peculiarly, a smell like that of scalded rubber.

As he toppled out of the cockpit, Ganelon saw the edge of the Bazonga bird's bronze wing go flashing past his face. Still clinging to the Silver Sword which the Nine Hegemons had given him in commemoration of his victory over the Indigons, he made a frantic snatch at the wing with his other hand.

His fingertips brushed against cold, hard bronze— clung—and held!

The bird-machine squawked deafeningly as Ganelon's weight caused it to sag heavily to port. It veered about in a wide, gliding circle, tipped crazily so that it was flying sideways through the sky. Xarda and the old magician clung to the sides of the cockpit, bracing themselves desperately. Xarda was shrieking and the Illusionist was cursing vehemently in thirty-seven ancient languages including nine that are spoken only on other planets and one that is chittered only by a race of intelligent insects who inhabit the center of the third moon of Saturn.

As for the Bazonga bird herself, she was unable to bring herself back to what might properly be termed an even keel. The magnetic waves by which the bird-vehicle propelled herself through the skies were evenly balanced in potency; sufficient to maintain the equilibrium of the metal bird during flight, they were not powerful enough to offset the immense unbalanced weight of the Construct.

And, as for Ganelon, he squeezed his eyes shut against the stinging winds and held on grimly, with the utmost tenacity of which his powerful fingers were capable. The strength of the giant's hand, several times that of the most powerfully developed human athlete, was enough to crumple the broad feathers of strong bronze into which the trailing edges of the stationary wings had been sculpted. The tough bronze crushed like a sheet of tinfoil in his grasp.

Ganelon stubbornly clung to his sword and tried futilely to return it to its scabbard. But the sword's case was between his shoulders, clipped to the broad leather strap of the baldric he wore, and it proved impossible for him to insert the point of the blade into the mouth of the scabbard without using his other hand to hold the end of the scabbard steady. There was no telling how long before the crushed wad of bronze feathertips would break cleanly away from the edge of the bird's wing, hurtling him two thousand feet to the jungles of Karjixia far below; and there was no way for him to pull himself up onto the broad level surface of the wing with the use of only one hand.

It was just about the most desperate situation in which the young giant had thus far found himself—a far worse predicament than merely fighting yerxels or Indigons or Horxite priests. Now was the time to think clearly, if ever he had needed to use the wits which the Illusionist had striven to train. Time and again his master had warned him that sheer strength and courage alone would not always be enough to bring him safely through a perilous situation, that he must learn to remain calm in an emergency and to think things out coolly and unhurriedly.

His fingers were not yet weary of the strain of supporting his entire weight; but before long they would begin to tire. Bronze is a tough and malleable metal, unlike steel, which is crystalline in structure and as often as not will break before it bends. He might have a minute or two left before the bronze handhold tore loose. Or he might have only seconds.

He opened his eyes, squinting against the wind that made them tear, and examined his predicament. First, he looked about, searching the sky for his adversary, who might well prove clever enough to realize that this was the best time to renew its attack. The Phlygûl, who seemed baffled by these peculiar goings-on, was circling the air vehicle warily; the Bazonga itself was circling, squawking hysterically all the while. It had not yet occurred to the poor creature that the best thing to do would be to land in the jungle as quickly as possible, before Ganelon fell to his death. What with all the noise of squawking, shrieking, and cursing, Ganelon probably could not get the bird's attention even were he to offer the suggestion in the most stentorian of voices.

The Phlygûl was beneath them now, staring up in a baffled manner, ogling the dangling giant who appeared as a tempting morsel, like a ripe fruit dangling at the end of a limb. Now the creature was directly under Silvermane. As he watched thoughtfully the batwinged creature maintained its position directly beneath him duplicating exactly the curve in which the frenzied Bazonga was flying.

Ganelon let go and fell like a stone—

Xarda screamed piercingly and closed her eyes in horror.

She opened them a moment later, for the Illusionist was shaking her by the shoulder. The bird swung violently back into its normal flight position, nearly tossing them over the starboard side; but now she was flying at an even keel again.

Xarda peered fearfully over the edge of the cockpit, dreading the sight of that splendid beautiful body slamming and battering down through the branches of the trees. Instead she beheld a sight very different from the one her imagination had painted.

Ganelon, still clinging to his sword, had landed on the back of the Phlygûl, who looked dazed and astounded. The impact of his fall would probably have knocked the wind out of the monster, if it breathed at all, which, lacking a nose, was probably not the case. Even as Xarda watched with wide, unbelieving eyes, the giant climbed up to a sitting position astride the base of the Phlygûl's neck, letting his legs dangle down to either side of its gaunt chest. Then he locked them about the base of the Phlygûl's throat, holding on to one of its brow-horns with his left hand. He grinned up at them with a flash of strong white teeth in his dark bronze face, waving the Silver Sword jubilantly.

The Phlygûl, doubtless, resented the imposition of an uninvited passenger, but not as furiously as Xarda might have expected. The creature reached up with gaunt, clawlike hands to clutch at the legs locked about its throat, but when it did Ganelon slapped them away with the flat of his sword. Then he slammed the sword-pommel a couple of times against the creature's black, bony skull, as if in stern reprimand. The creature blinked dazedly, but accepted the presence of the giant with a degree of surly docility that astounded the girl knight—until it occurred to her that, after all, the Airmasters themselves used the Phlygûl for riding purposes. So, now that she thought of it, the Phlygûl was probably accustomed to bearing a rider on its back and the experience was not an unfamiliar one.

Ganelon quickly got used to his remarkable flying steed. He discovered that by seizing hold of the forward-curving horn that sprouted from the middle of the monster's forehead, and jerking its head around to the right or the left, he could make the creature fly in whatever direction he wanted.

Waving at his friends aloft, he gestured in the direction

of Sky Island, now only a dozen miles distant. And as the
Bazonga resumed its course, he followed all the way to
Sky Island on his batwinged aerial steed.

The island proved to be a fairly good-sized bit of land,
about ten miles in circumference. Most of it was covered
with dense jungles, but toward the northern edge rose
rocky hills. From the looks of those hills, the caverns tun-
neled into them, the washing sheds and barracks built before them, it was obvious that the Airmasters mined them
for metals.

The capital of the Sky Islanders was a town of red
brick and yellow stone, rather on the small side. It boasted
an immense and elaborately ornamented palace, or temple, or perhaps a combination of both; and the town was
unwalled, although a high wooden palisade had been erected along the edge of the island nearest to the town. Obviously this had been built to prevent the children of the Sky
Islanders from getting too close to the edge and either falling over or being blown over by the cold winds that blew
rather strongly at this height. There was a medium-sized
lake some little distance from the town which looked to be
man-made. This was probably a reservoir built to catch
and retain rainwater.

The air at this height was clear and pretty cold, but not
as frigid as one might have thought. Still, it was curious to
find a tropical jungle, obviously a flourishing one, at such
a height. As the Illusionist pointed out, however, there was
no way of telling how many millions of years the island
had been floating in the skies above Old Earth. Perhaps
the jungle vegetation had gradually adapted to the chill-
iness over half an Eon or so.

The Bazonga bird landed toward the middle of the island, where an odd-looking structure reared above the
treetops; and Ganelon brought his ungainly and monstrous
steed down nearby, although the creature protested with
irritable squeakings. Dismounting to rejoin his comrades,
he released the creature, which flapped out of sight.

"It seems to want to land atop that tall, many-tiered
tower near the palace-temple," said Silvermane. The magician nodded.

"I noticed, as we came in view of the city, that you
seemed to be having trouble keeping the Phlygûl under
control," he observed. "Perhaps that is the aviary wherein

the Phlygûl are housed when not in use; the several tiers were each lined with circular apertures which might lead to the Phlygûl nests, or roosts, or whatever."

"Why did you insist on landing so far in the interior of Sky Island, Magister?" asked the Sirix of Jemmerdy. "The city itself must be a couple of miles from here."

"For one thing, I think it best that we approach the city of the Airmasters unobserved, able to scrutinize it from a place of concealment such as the jungle's edge," said the Illusionist. "For another, I am curious as to the nature and purpose of this odd structure, built so far from the city and situated, you will observe, at the exact mathematical center of Sky Island. Come, let us reconnoiter."

"And what shall I do?" inquired the Bazonga bird. The amusing creature seemed bound and determined to share the adventure with them as an equal partner.

"You? You can keep one eye peeled for unexpected company," said the magician. "If any of the Airmasters approach, they will probably do so by air; so watch out for Phlygûl and give a screech if you see one."

The bird acquiesced and began staring fixedly at the sky. They made their way toward the peculiar, towerlike structure. It was raised in the center of a roughly circular glade or meadow that was surrounded by a wall of jungle and bore every sign of having been artificially cleared. As they approached the spire they saw that it was a tall shaft of sparkling blue metal, topped by a polished sphere of what looked like shining brass or copper. The base of the shaft was concealed in a boxlike enclosure of solid metal. It was windowless and had a circular door, also of metal; the door looked as strong as the door to a bank vault. They paused before this enigmatic portal and examined it curiously.

Ganelon craned his head intently. "Do you hear that humming, throbbing sound?" he asked. "It sounds like an enormous beehive, coupled with a beating heart...."

"No, my boy. Your hearing is more acute than ours; but I smell ozone, and that means electricity. Whatever is inside that door, there is at least some sort of an engine or motor within. A power source, then ... but for what?"

Ganelon reached out and took hold of the handles on the vaultlike door. Great bands of muscle swelled along his back and arms and shoulders. From the massive hinges and lock-mechanism of the door there came the screech of tortured metal.

"I think I can open it with just a little—" he began. But he did not finish the sentence. For suddenly, from vents unobtrusively set in the walls about the door, jets of vapor were released. A white mist eddied about them, vanishing almost instantly. And in the same moment an alarm light began flashing atop the boxlike structure.

"Phlygûl approaching! Hey, there! *Hoy!* Phlygûl are coming from the city with riders on their backs!" shrieked the Bazonga from the edge of the jungle. But the three figures sprawled motionless about the unopened door did not answer.

24.

THE MAN ENTIRELY
CLOTHED IN GOLD

When they awoke they had dull, throbbing headaches and a sour, brassy taste in their mouths. They peered blearily about at stone walls and benches; they were stretched out on the latter, and their wrists had been chained behind them. They had been stripped of everything except their clothing and ornaments: all weapons, tools, purses, or pouches were gone. Xarda still wore her breastplates, abbreviated chainmesh skirt, greaves and gorget, but her lovely longsword, dirk, poniard, and small ax were missing. A pity, she thought, for they had been a perfectly matched set, and a bargain at that. Ganelon was still attired in his war-harness of black leather straps, girdle, and scarlet loincloth; but his sword and pouch were missing.

He sat up with a grunt and began testing his manacles. They were fashioned of a dark, heavy metal he did not recognize. His face screwed into a painful grimace; his brows blackened with effort. But the chains, surprisingly, did not break or even give in the slightest.

"Save your strength, my boy; the chains are of adamant

and it would take far more strength than even you possess to burst them asunder," the Illusionist said in somber tones.

Xarda looked about wonderingly.

"How did we get here? And, for that matter, where are we? That white vapor—"

"A sleep-inducing vapor, obviously," replied the Illusionist. "Hush! Someone is coming!"

Ten men entered the stone room through a door that was itself a slab of granitelike substance. The men were tall, supplely built, lean, and hawk-faced. Their heads were shaved bare and they wore winged helmets of sparkling transparent crystal. Their torsos were covered by silken tunics of sky-blue weave, ending at mid-thigh, leaving their legs also bare. They wore greaves and gauntlets, or rigid cuffs, anyway, of the same crystalline material. Each bore naked in his left hand a peculiar tubular sword from whose hilt a copper wire snaked to a power-pack affixed to a waist belt. Sparks crackled about the sharp tips of these weapons, whose blades sizzled ominously.

"Do not resist the warriors, Ganelon, for they are armed with electric swords!" cautioned the Illusionist. Ganelon glowered at them, grumbling, but permitted the Airmasters to haul him to his feet without quarrel.

The three prisoners were taken from the detention cubicle down a long, narrow corridor and into an immense domed hall thronged with beautiful, bejeweled women in glittering gowns and languid, haughty men exquisitely clothed and scented. The prevailing colors worn by the assemblage were sky-blue, silver, gray, and black. Winged insignia were everywhere, emblazoned on tabard and jupon, cloak and tunic, painted on shield, helmet, and wall, carved above doorways and on the backs of chairs, set with tessellated tiles into the mosaiclike floor, and woven on flags and bannerols. They knew without words that these haughty, glittering nobles were the Airmasters.

The guards who had led them into this immense hall now conducted them through the throng to the center of the room, where a figure sat enshrined in a gigantic throne atop a towering cylinder. The guards knelt on all fours as they neared this cylindrical dais and intoned in unison:

"On your faces before The First Elphod! Grovel at the feet of the Voice of Gulnazphaz, Smiter of the Horxite Heretics, Terror of All Infidels, Beloved of the Gods!"

Ganelon growled and spat. "I grovel to nothing that lives!" he said. Then, lifting his eyes to the motionless figure atop the cylinder, his eyes widened and he gasped.

It was the figure of a man clothed entirely in gold. The golden mask that concealed his features was carved in the likeness of superhuman beauty, majesty, grimness. A huge, togalike robe covered most of his body and limbs; this was of pure gold chainmesh. Gauntlets of solid gold encased his hands; boots of solid gold encased his feet. Directly above him, sunlight poured down from a circular opening in the dome, bathing him in brilliant radiance. The mirrorlike metal wherewith he was entirely covered reflected this light in an aura of dazzling brilliance that was intolerable and blinding.

From the mouth-slit in the golden mask came faint, rasping breath, speaking as if with great effort.

"They do not grovel. Let them be beaten until they do."

Grim-faced guards strode forward purposefully, but the Illusionist forestalled them. He laughed, and said amusedly, "By the Red Obelisk, Vlydabec, you old rascal, but you have certainly risen in the world! Can you even move under all that metal, or do people have to pick you up and carry you about like a piece of furniture?"

The jape must have been at least a first-degree blasphemy, for a horrified gasp went up and, with a single movement, like a field full of flowers bending before a strong wind, all that bejeweled and silken throng sank to the floor on their faces and lay motionless. Even the guards, approaching to chastise them, paled with terror and fell flat—obviously expecting lightning bolts to blast the impertinent speaker to flinders in the next instant.

This, however, did not transpire. After a moment or two of stunned silence, a thin, querulous voice issued from the golden thing on the throne.

"Who addresses the First Elphod in such familiar terms?" it quavered weakly. "Who names us with the former name we have set behind us since our Revelation and Apotheosis? Speak!"

"One who remembers you from the old days, when we were schoolmates together at Nembosch, studying the Sixty Sciences. I recall we used to make fun of your long nose and admirable rash of pimples. I also remember we used to call you 'Stinky' Vlydabec, because you did not bathe frequently enough. Remember the time 'Rat-Tooth' Quilf and 'Sneezer' Ibsthic threw you in the well and told you not to come out until you'd made up for the last fourteen baths you had missed?" The Illusionist sniggered: it was a remarkable sound, considering the deathlike silence that reigned over the shuddering throng who lay on their faces, trembling with horror, unable to believe their ears.

"S-silence, blasphemer!" shrilled a weak, ancient voice from behind the imperturbable golden mask. With immense effort one hand, gloved in solid gold, raised itself about three inches from the arm of the throne and sternly waggled one forefinger. The gold-clad finger quivered violently with the effort it took to make the gesture.

"Who is this m-madman, and where was the vile infidel taken?" wheezed the faint voice through the mouth-slit of the gold mask.

One of the guards, stretched out on his belly in terror, said something in a faint voice.

"Speak up, worm!" said the golden image.

The frightened soldier cleared his throat and repeated the explanation more clearly.

"The intruders were tampering with the door of the Death Machine, Holy Prophet," he said. "We are uncertain as to how they managed to reach the isle; doubtless they have their vehicle hidden somewhere in the jungle, but we have not found it as yet."

"The Death Machine, you say?" quavered the weak voice. Whoever was concealed behind the golden armor sounded worried and agitated. "Did the impious and sinful snakes manage to effect an entry? Is the Machine tampered with?"

"No, Divinity. The portal is still sealed; they were overcome by the Sleep Vapor before managing to damage the mechanism of the lock."

"I deduce from your terminology, as well as by your agitation, that the spirelike structure is the controlling instrument by which you cause the Death Zone to move about," said the Illusionist, interrupting at this point. "I had thought as much from the fact that it had been built at the exact center of the island, and thus stood at the nexus of the gravitational forces of Sky Island. It is really very naughty of you, Vlydabec, you old scoundrel, to cause the poor, inoffensive Tigermen so much trouble and aggravation; but then I seem to recall that you were always creating dissension, even back at school. What a

nasty boy you were! Such a troublemaker! Remember the
time our tutor in Higher Thaumaturgy threatened to
transform you into a slimy green toad if you would not
promise to cease bullying' and tormenting the younger,
weaker boys—"

· The stiff seated figure clad in gold hissed and stuttered
in a paroxysm of fury. Rheumy old eyes glittered evilly
through the eye-slits in the mask. They were hard and
cold and ugly, those eyes, and deadly: like globs of frozen
venom, Ganelon thought. Despite himself, the Construct
felt a shiver of disgust and chill apprehension run through
his mighty frame. The thing in the gold armor had once
been human, doubtless; but a lifetime devoted to the lust
of power and dominance over the minds and bodies—and
even the souls—of other men had drained the essential humanity from it long ago. Now the ancient was filled with
cold greed and its ego was a great, swollen, diseased thing.

No wonder Master called this Elphod one of the most
dangerous things in YamaYamaLand, thought Ganelon.

The First Elphod was fairly quivering with supressed
rage, spluttering feebly but viciously. The Airmasters of
his court lay groveling on their bellies, scarcely daring to
breathe the same air. The existence in their halls of so irreverent a blasphemer, they believed, tainted and polluted
everything it touched. Ganelon could read their panic, and
grim, contemptuous way it amused him.

Or would have amused him had the situation not been
quite so desperate.

Finally, the spluttering voice managed to find the power
of articulate speech again.

"S-such obscenities befoul the very air sanctified by our
blessed presence," hissed the man dressed entirely in gold.
Through the eye-slits of his mask, the weak and watery
eyes glared with maniacal rage.

"What punishment does Your Holiness decree for such
audacious and incredible blasphemy?" whispered the
leader of the guards with trembling lips.

The eyes brooded behind the mask, judiciously considering and rejecting a variety of curious and intricate tor-
ments. Then they flashed with the dreadful glitter of cold,
gloating cruelties.

"Let them be dismembered slowly under the Whirling
Knives, and their tissues reduced in the protein tanks to

provide nutriment for our table," whispered the man entirely clothed in gold.

Ganelon's stomach muscles tightened in revulsion at the thought. But there was nothing he could do to prevent the doom levied against them. For even he could not break the adamantine chains that bound his wrists!

25.

THE THING THAT GLOWED IN THE DARK

The golden statuelike figure stirred fretfully, or, rather, tried to stir. The glittering mail was obviously so heavy that it was all the old man could do merely to breathe under the crushing weight of the soft metal.

"We are offended at such iniquities, such verbal obscenities, uttered in our presence," the quavering voice complained petulantly. "Guardsmen: take these vile atheists away and dispose of their tissues as we have instructed. Now we shall withdraw the ineffable bliss and benison of our sacred person from this befouled and tainted place ... the priests are instructed to cleanse and purify it with prayer and suffumigations for seven days. Only then shall we again enrich and bless this assemblage by resuming the sacred throne."

As the feeble voice ceased speaking, lights began to play upon the motionless figure from several unseen sources. The intensity of the rays increased rapidly; soon the golden figure blazed with blinding dazzle. Every square inch of the figure was covered like an idol with pure gold, highly polished, reflective as a mirror. The dazzling radiance became intolerable, sunlike. Even Ganelon Silvermane was forced to squeeze his eyes shut against such incandescence.

A moment later the blaze of golden glory dimmed, faded, and was gone.

They opened their eyes cautiously, blinking to dispel the vibrant blue afterimages. And saw to their astonishment that the huge throne was now completely empty. The figure of the Elphod had vanished; it was as if he had melted into vapor and dispersed into thin air. And yet he could hardly move a finger under the weight of all that gold; how, then, had he managed to leave the throne atop the tall, thick pedestal?

It was uncanny; it was just a little frightening. Ganelon could not understand it. And, as for the girl knight at his side, she was wide-eyed with amazement.

"By my halidom," swore Xarda, 'but how did he manage to get away without our seeing him? Was it a real miracle?"

"Tush!" the Illusionist snorted. "Mere sleight-of-hand, my child. The sort of thing we learned in the first semester of Stage Trickery 107, back at school! The light blinded us and made us all look away while the throne sank into the hollow pedestal on an hydraulic lift. Then waiting slaves carried him out of the chair and let it reascend to the top of the pedestal quite empty, in time for us to see. A matter of clever timing, nothing more!"

The assemblage rose and dispersed; the guards led them away.

The interview was over.

They were given food and water before being returned to their cell. The food was a lukewarm, greasy stew composed of a few unappetizing lumps of some unidentifiable meat, floating in a dish half filled with tasteless gravy. The water, however, was cold and fresh.

Since their hands were still bound behind them, the guards had to spoon the slop into their mouths. Ganelon ate the congealing mess indifferently; it was well past the middle of the day and he was hungry. In view of their sentence, however, he did have a few second thoughts about those lumps of meat. He rather queasily hoped they were not portions of one of yesterday's convicted heretics, reduced in the protein vats!

That also caused him to reflect on the peculiar behavior of the Sky Islanders. Why would they feed a man they were about to slice up with Whirling Knives? The illogic of lunchtime just before execution so baffled and intrigued him that, dodging the next-to-last spoonful, he asked the guard about it.

The fellow shrugged. "The hour is not auspicious for execution of His Holiness' instructions concerning you," the fellow said callously. "It is now the Hour of the Toad—a vile, ill-omened part of the day; and the Hour of the Worm, which follows next, is little better. The Augurs report that not until the hour after sundown will the time be ripe for the dissolution of your tissues."

Xarda gagged just then on the lump of tissue she had been chewing. Obviously the notion that had earlier occurred to Ganelon had just occurred to her. Their meal finished, they were led back to their cell. It was the same stone-walled chamber in which they had awakened after their recovery from the sleep-inducing vapor which had overcome them at the portal to the Death Machine.

Xarda looked pale and queasy, and just a trifle green about the gills. She cast a suffering glance at Silvermane.

"You would have to ask that q-question about the d-dissolution of our tissues just then, wouldn't you?" she asked in a feeble little voice.

"Oh, tut! Cheer up, my lass!" advised the Illusionist in a cheery tone. "At least we have all afternoon to digest that greasy slop they pushed in our faces. We now know that the jolly old Whirling Knives have been postponed until the hour after sundown. There's good news, eh? Goodness knows what might occur between now and then!"

At the hearty ring in his joking words, the girl steeled herself. Her lips tightened and the muscles along her jaw bunched purposively. Chivalry demanded that she put a good face on things and stiffen her upper lip, ready for come-what-may. If the old magician could face the imminent dissolution of his tissues with equanimity, so, by Galendil, could she!

"That's the spirit, girl," he chirped. "Never say die!"

The guards opened the cell door and thrust them inside hurriedly, sliding the stone slab back into place. It sealed the portal with a heavy grating thump, and they were alone.

The Illusionist went over to one of the stone benches and sat down. Although he grumbled a bit at the difficulties of sitting comfortably with his hands manacled behind his back, he seemed to be actually enjoying their predicament in some curious way. Ganelon could not help noticing that his spirits seemed to have risen ever since their capture; he had tossed disparaging remarks at the Holy Elphod with a flippant zest which Ganelon thought remarkable. What the young giant did not realize was that to the Illusionist, who had lived many centuries in conditions of comfort and even luxury, genuine danger and peril broke the monotony deliciously, and he found himself enjoying the hazardous confrontation with heady gusto.

But something else was puzzling Silvermane.

"Master," he said, "I didn't know you had been a schoolmate of the Elphod's; you never mentioned anything about having known him before. . . ."

"Quite right, and for the very good reason that I have never before laid eyes on the fellow," the Illusionist replied. "The Horxites maintain excellently detailed and thoroughly researched personal dossiers on their major heretics. This data, plus a bit of scrying in my wizard's crystal, produced quite a few scurrilous items of interest from old Vlydabec's unsavory past. Oh, I studied at Nembosch once; but that was long before the old fool was even born. I am older than you think me, boy!"

Xarda was working grimly on her manacles, but gave up with a gusty sigh. "If only I could free my hands! And find my sword!" she said wistfully.

"Calm yourself, my child," said the Illusionist.

She uttered a most unladylike snort of derision. "Calm myself, is it? How can you just sit there, when in a few hours they will be reducing our tissues to bubbling slime in the protein tanks? *Ugh!*" She shivered. "The very thought congeals my marrow!"

"No doubt. But, as for myself, I am going to enjoy a brief nap. It has been a fairly exciting day, all things considered. And I advise you to do the same: conserve your strength and energy for a later moment, when we shall need everything that is within us." With that the Illusionist stretched out on the bench, kicked and wriggled until he was laying on his side, and composed himself for slumber. Ganelon obediently did the same; after a while, Xarda gave up struggling against her manacles and lay down, too, worn out from the hectic furor of the day.

Quite a while later Ganelon came suddenly awake, nerves tingling with alarm. His phloigms, more sensitive than those of the girl, who still lay sound asleep, warned him of the presence of a dangerous supernatural creature.

He craned his neck in order to look around—and froze in shock!

A strange, towering figure stood in the cell. It glowed in the dark with an eerie red light, and it was in nowise human. Ganelon caught only a blurred, swift glimpse of the thing: only enough to see that it had clumsy, monstrous limbs instead of human arms or hands and that it was clad in strange, uncouth armor, red as blood.

It was bending over the Illusionist, who still slept on, oblivious to the menacing apparition!

Then Ganelon was on his feet somehow, howling and roaring, and charging to his master's defense. Although what he could do to fight the monster with his hands behind him, he did not know.

26.

TO THE DEATH MACHINE

There was no way to battle the strange monster who glowed in the dark and who had appeared among them like an apparition, so Ganelon butted it in the pit of the stomach with his head. That is, he butted it in the place where its stomach would be, if it had possessed a stomach, which it happened not to.

The blow, however, did not seem to cause the armored monster any appreciable amount of discomfort. It did, however, rather daze the giant himself for a few wobbly moments. And it also managed to awaken the dormant headache he had from the aftereffects of breathing the sleep vapor.

He groaned and backed off and tried to give it a kick with his booted foot.

"Get away from my master, you hideous monster!" he growled.

Why you cuss at poor Fryx so? asked Fryx in a hurt tone of voice (or thought, rather, since the Gyraphont communicated by telepathy). *Why you bump head on thorax of Fryx?* the creature continued in the same vein. *You crazy boy, mebee? Fryx no like you no more; no bring you cocoa in bed no more, crazy boy, kick Fryx with foot! You bad boy.*

"Fryx? Fryx!" Silvermane mumbled numbly. He blinked his bleary gaze clear and took a closer look at the hulking thing. Now, of course, he recognized the chitinous red lobster-thing with its multiple limbs and pincers. He ought to have remembered that Fryx glowed in the dark; it was just something that Gyraphonts did.

"*Fryx!* What are you doing here, Fryx?" he asked, bewildered.

Master call, Fryx come, is all. Crazy bad boy!

"But—why are you here? I mean—"

"Because I called him, of course. Simpleton!" sniffed the Illusionist, sitting up and turning about so that Fryx could snip through his manacles with those huge lobsterlike pincers of his. Being a supernatural entity, Fryx could apply superhuman strength to the cutting of even adamantine chains.

"Called him? But I thought you were asleep!"

"I let you think that to spare you the pangs of perhaps false hope," said the Illusionist, "in case I failed, that is. I have never before had occasion to try to mentally summon Fryx to my side over such a very great distance. I am not a natural telepath, although of course I have had to learn the art for my work. But one thing helped me, and that was that Fryx was already attuned to my wavelength and alert and ready for summons. I arranged that before we left Nerelon."

Ganelon shook his head as if to get his brains working again. Then he turned about so that Fryx could snip away his chains, having finished freeing the wrists of the Illusionist.

Xarda sat backed against the wall, staring at them, eyes huge and fearful. She was not quite certain the frightening red monster with the thirteen eyes was really friendly, being able to hear only one side of the exchange, since

Fryx was not broadcasting to her, having not yet noticed she was also in the room.

"It's all right, my dear; Fryx is a servant of mine, a bit of a pet, and quite an old friend," the Illusionist said cheerily.

Who pretty lady? Fryx inquired, bending six or seven eyes upon her with curiosity. *Mebbe she you girl frien', hey, crazy boy?* the creature asked maliciously. Ganelon blinked uncomprehendingly; Xarda flushed crimson and bit her lip.

A few moments later Fryx had removed the chains from all three of them and they stood, gratefully rubbing their aching wrists.

"Things look quite a bit brighter now than they did before we all had our little nap." The Illusionist grinned. "It still lacks almost an hour of our appointment with the Whirling Knives; I'm afraid, however, that the jolly old protein tanks are going to be kept waiting this night. Fryx, I want you to take me to the spire that stands at the exact center of Sky Island, leave me there, and come back for Ganelon and this young lady; do you understand me?"

Hokay said Fryx amicably. The magician took hold of the Gyraphont's upper forefront limb and both of them promptly vanished. Xarda turned green and gulped. Never before had the Chivalric Code of Jemmerdy been so severely taxed!

Guessing the general tenor of her thoughts, Ganelon said comfortingly, "It's not unpleasant to go between the dimensions, Xarda. I've done it myself with Fryx a couple of times."

"Oh, I believe you!" she said, with a slight shudder. "It's just that I shall never get accustomed to the way you two travel about. That flying bronze bird-thing that argues with the Magister all the time, well, he was bad enough—"

"She," corrected Ganelon.

"All right, *she* was bad enough. I had just about got used to flying in a talkative metal thing, when you decide to finish off the trip on the back of a black, rubbery, obscene bat-monster with a thirty-foot wingspread. And now you expect me to pop out of existence somehow in the clutches of a Gyraphont! Oh, none of my sister-knights will ever believe this when I get back to Jemmerdy," she said. "*If* I get back to Jemmerdy, that is," she added by way of an afterthought.

Fryx melted out of thin air at Ganelon's side, and did it so suddenly that Xarda gasped and jumped an inch in the air, then hated herself for doing so.

You ready! No kick old Fryx, now!

"No, of course I won't, Fryx. Fryx, I'm awfully sorry. I thought you were a—" Ganelon got only partly through his apologies when Fryx took him gently by the arm and did whatever it is that Gyraphonts do in order to take a shortcut across space by dodging between the dimensions. Ganelon vanished in mid-explanation. And then it was Xarda's turn.

Night had fallen; the stars flashed and twinkled in the heavens above Sky Island, appreciably bigger and more brilliant than when seen from the planet's surface.

The blue metal spire of the Death Machine gleamed with oily highlights in the glimmering of the Falling Moon. The harsh stench of ozone was sharp as iodine. Sparks crackled faintly from the brass ball atop the blue shaft, and they could faintly hear the drone and throb of engines from within the structure.

"If we can manage to wreck this installation before our escape is discovered, we will destroy the ability of the Airmasters to levy tribute from Karjixia and its neighboring realms," said the Illusionist. "Somehow or other this machine controls the movements of the Death Zone."

"But if I try to break open the vault-door, won't the sleep vapor render us unconscious again?" asked Ganelon.

The magician nodded affably. "Yes, but we won't break in and trip the gas-releasing mechanism." The veiled magician turned to the lobster-creature. "Fryx, I want you to enter the interior of this structure by your shortcut method and open the vault-door from inside. Do you think you can do that?"

The Gyraphont blinked eight or nine eyes thoughtfully. *Hokay.* He promptly vanished and the three adventurers retreated some distance in order to get beyond the range of the sleep-inducing gas, should Fryx perchance trip the mechanism by mistake. They stood in the starlight waiting for the door to open.

"I wonder how these fanatics got their conqueror-complex in the first place," murmured Xarda, nervously hefting her sword. Fryx had located and rescued their weapons in between trips. "I thought they were just a dissident cult. . . ."

"They started off that way," said the Illusionist. "They fled to Sky Island to avoid Horxite persecution, and to worship in the way they pleased. Nothing wrong with that at all, commendable, in fact. But before long they began to change; fanatics are always vulnerable to the sin of overweening pride, you know. The I-am-holier-than-thou atttitude is dangerous and corrupting. Living here in the sky they were closer to the Gods than their earthbound brethren, and soon started thinking themselves naturally superior to the dwellers beneath. Living in the heavens like Gods, it was not long before they began believing they were more like the Gods than those who lived below on Old Earth. The tribute they exact from the poor Tigermen is psychologically the same thing as exacting worship from an inferior species, I would say. Unless we stop them now, they will subjugate Karjixia; then Phynx and Yombok and Quay, and Ixland and the Horxites, and half the countries around. A religious empire—a theocracy—run by a fanatical old madman who regards other men as vile infidels, fit only to serve his own holiness as groveling slaves. Not a pretty picture of the future, is it?"

"I wonder what's keeping Fryx," grumbled Ganelon.

"Yoo-hoo! People!" called a voice from the edge of the jungle. They turned as the Bazonga bird floated into view, emerging partway from the foliage to peer about tentatively.

"So there you are," said the magician. "I wondered where you had got to."

"You all decided to take a nap," said the bird-vehicle severely, "and wouldn't wake up when I called. Then the bat-people came and there was nothing for me to do but hide until they went away. I'm afraid I'm not very good at adventures," she confessed.

"Nonsense, my dear vehicle," the Illusionist tried to comfort her. "It is, after all, your first adventure, and you were never constructed with battles in mind. Not your fault at all; and very wise of you to seek a hiding place rather than let yourself be captured. A very intelligent move!"

"Oh, do you really think so? How nice! I was afraid you'd be angry with little me," the bird simpered. Despite the tension of waiting for Fryx, Xarda could not help giggling at the ridiculous but lovable creature.

"*Hoy!*" Ganelon boomed suddenly. "There we are!" The vault-door had just swung open, this time without releasing the protective jets of anesthetic gas.

"Good old Fryx," said the Illusionist, rubbing his hands together briskly as they hurried up to the door. The lobster-being lurked within anxiously.

Fryx do hokay? Take long time to figger out, he said. They assured him he had performed his task splendidly. The magician peered inside at the curiously designed engines and motors; tall vacuum tubes lit by glowing filaments loomed in the dark interior; circuit breakers crackled and clicked. On one wall a complicated control board flashed with indicator lights.

"This will take a bit of thinking through," the magician said briskly. "You stand here and guard the entrance while I busy myself inside. If attacked, Fryx will help you, I am sure. Hold off any attackers as long as you can; I will be too busy within to help you."

He vanished within, closing the vault-door. Ganelon leaned on the Silver Sword, looking around alertly.

And then, without warning, Airmaster soldiers burst from every side of the jungle clearing and charged the Death Machine, shouting and brandishing weapons. In the next instant, Ganelon and Xarda were fighting for their lives.

27.

THE BATTLE AT WORLD'S END

Never had their been so weird and marvelous a battle scene in all the years of Old Earth! In a jungle clearing on a floating island, miles above the planet's surface, Ganelon Silvermane and the knightrix of Jemmerdy fought with flashing blades against a howling horde of crystal-armored

Airmasters, and only the great, glaring eye of the Falling Moon peered down to watch the uncanny scene.

To either side of the two there fought beside them perhaps the strangest allies ever leagued with man in all his many wars. To one side loomed the glowing, scarlet-shelled figure of the lobster-ghoul, his thirteen eyes glimmering through the dark, his monstrous claws and pincers snapping and flailing. To the other, floated the sentient vehicle of weightless bronze, squawking its queer war-cry, bowling over the enemy warriors with invisible rays of magnetic force.

Starlight flickered in Silvermane's flowing, unearthly mane and the silver glory of the Falling Moon flashed and dazzled in the mirror-brightness of his magic sword. He fought tirelessly, booming the deep-throated war-cries of the Zermishmen, and his great sword splintered through crystal helm, cuirass, and shield, biting deep in flesh and bone. Like some primal champion, some savage giant from Time's Dawn, he fought there on the threshold of the Death Machine, battling with supernal vigor in the Twilight of Time.

No less heroically did the girl knight of Jemmerdy fight at his side. Her small, stubborn chin lifted defiantly, her green eyes flashing with battle-joy, red locks floating on the breeze, the slim, lithe girl struck and parried and struck again. The thin-bladed Jemmerdine longsword looked like a child's toy next to the giant's Silver Sword, but it was cunningly fashioned of thin strong supple steel, and its razor edges and needle-point reaped a gory harvest of the foe, who lay heaped before Xarda like sheaves of wheat fallen before the reaper's scythe. As she fought, the girl knight lifted her clear young voice in a joyous war-song that in old days had rung out upon a thousand battlefields of warlike Jemmerdy:

> *The bright steel flashes, swift and strong!*
> *And cleaves a red road through the throng!*
> *Come, warriors, lift your voice in song—*
> *For Jemmerdy! Jemmerdy!*

Before the battle was thirty minutes old, the guardsmen of the Airmasters began to falter. Never before had they actually fought a battle, preferring to swagger through the halls of their citadel in immaculate tunics and polished crystal mail. The sweat and blood and pain of real fighting was something new to them and they soon found they did not like it. Arms and shoulders whose soft sinews had heretofore only known the pleasant, limited exercise of practice field and swordsmen's school now ached in weary earnest. Stinking sweat ran down their chests under sticky, soiled tunics; they began to pant with exhaustion, and every breath was painful in their dry throats.

The silver-haired giant towered above them like a mighty colossus hewn of cold bronze. His gigantic thews stood out in bold relief, edged with moonlight. His terrible sword cut them down by the dozens, and no three of them were strong enough to stand before him for long. Even the shock and sparkle of their electric swords did not seem to stop or even slow him; he grunted, sucking in his breath, at the stinging, numbing touches. But the vitality of Ganelon Silvermane was many times that of ordinary men, and the shocks that would have paralyzed any other warrior of Old Earth were to him little more than the discomforts inflicted by stinging gnats. With his great length of arm, and the extra length afforded by the Silver Sword, few and seldom were the Airmasters who got close enough to the tireless warrior to so much as give him a grazing blow.

As for the girl knight of Jemmerdy, she was in her element and gloried in the flickering, rapierlike play of guard and thrust and parry. Her nimble agility and the dexterity with which she eluded their blows to sink her own swift, darting point in arm or throat or thigh of adversaries made it all but impossible for them to so much as touch her with their power blades. Defeat at the brilliant swordsmanship of a laughing, bright-eyed girl made them tremble and bluster with impotent fury, confusing the Airmasters and spoiling their timing—an advantage the clever girl soon spotted and took great advantage of.

As for the weird bronze bird-machine, caroling wild, harsh cries of "Tally-ho" and "Yoicks," she knocked the soldiers over like tenpins with her shooting waves of impalpable force. Bracing her fan-spread tail squarely against the side of the metal building, the Bazonga beat back and hurled aside the charging Sky Islanders with those magnetic force tubes that pointed to her front and had been designed to brake or slow her forward flight. There were no means by which the Airmasters could have slain or injured the enormous bronze creature, even had they been able to get within reach of her; many were the broken limbs and wounds her powerful darting rays inflicted upon the foe in that weird battle above the world.

Neither could Fryx be harmed or injured. Although made of flesh, his tough, chitinous armor was stronger even than steel, and armed as he was with those terrible huge lobster-claws, the faithful Gyraphont took a mighty toll of their opponents on that corpse-strewn field. Those mighty pincers crunched through blade or arm or helm alike, and the very sight of the monstrous, supernatural creature struck terror into the souls of the superstitious fanatics who fought against him, making their blows weak and tentative and sapping their courage and fortitude.

They fought on, bathed in the unearthly silver splendor of the enormous Moon, the mysterious shaft of the Death Machine soaring behind them against the ageless stars. Perhaps never in all the immeasurable eons of time had those cool and timeless stars looked down on a stranger battle, fought in a stranger place, for a stranger and more desperate cause.

Even from the beginning it was an unfair contest. Even from the start the outcome was doubtful. They were only four, the defenders of the helpless people of Gondwane, and the soldiers of Sky Island against whom they fought so stubbornly and so tirelessly were counted in the hundreds.

For a time they held firm against the foe. But only for a time.

The first to fall was Xarda. The girl knight of Jemmerdy was only human, after all. Although she was young and strong and daring, with a cool head, a steely wrist, and a brilliant swordswoman with the consummate skill and courage that would have daunted many men, she had not the superhuman strength and tireless vitality that drove the mighty giant at her side.

Suddenly she strove to hold at bay six Sky Island soldiers at once. The greatest master swordsman of all time might have failed against those grim odds. It says much for Xarda of Jemmerdy that she held firm against their flickering power blades for six minutes. To her they seemed six measureless eternities. Three of her foemen she stretched at her feet in rivering gore. But then, simultaneously engaging the points of two of her remaining adversaries, she left herself momentarily unguarded against a third. His sizzling tubular blade flew past her ward to strike at her head. Even in that last extremity of effort she glided to one side, avoiding the full force of the stroke. But the energy sword struck her a glancing blow on the temple.

The numbing electric shock wrung the strength from her. Stunned and reeling, she let her longsword fall from nerveless fingers. She crumpled to her knees, fighting against the impalpable darkness that surged up to drown her consciousness. Then a sword-point struck her unguarded brow. The shock of it drove splinters of incandescence through her brain and she fell to one side and knew no more.

Beside the steps of the Death Machine installation, Ganelon fought on tirelessly, grimly, his sword-strokes rising and falling like the unwearying pistons of some powerful fighting machine. Seeing the fall of Xarda, the giant swung roaring and disemboweled the four men who had struck her down with one wide slashing stroke of the Silver Sword. It was silver no longer, that magical blade: from point to quillon it was slick and wet and scarlet.

He took up a new stance, standing over the fallen girl, guarding her with his own body. And he fought on, grim and tenacious and stubbornly unyielding. His chest and arms and mighty shoulders were scored with many wounds by now; blood trickled from many places on his magnificent torso. He hardly felt the pain, for the red fury of battle-joy possessed him utterly. *I was born for this*, he thought to himself dimly through the roaring tumult; *born to fight and fall in the defense of True Men. I am not even human. What does my death matter, after all?*

Still, it troubled him. He did not fear death in the least, but he begrudged the Dark Kingdom of the Shadows its victory. It was not right or just that he should die here, never having discovered the reason for which he had been born. . . .

He glanced to one side of him, aware that the joyous war-whoops of the Bazonga bird had died away. The bronze machine, still weightless, now floated dead and lifeless. No more did the terrible magnetic rays shoot from the base of its throat and the forward edges of its rigid wings to scatter and buffet the enemy. Its eye-lenses were dull and unaware now. The toil of battle had drained its supplies of energy, thought Ganelon dully to himself.

He glanced over to his left. But Fryx was no longer there; his place was empty. Had the Gyraphont tasted fear at last, and fled into the strange places between the dimensions, where the soldiers could never follow him? Poor Fryx! But he could not fault the faithful creature for deserting a lost cause, and saving himself.

Ganelon drew in a deep breath. Even his tremendous strength was ebbing now, as it had ebbed toward the last in the battle against the Indigons. His shoulders ached; his arms were weary; and all the while blood leaked slowly from the many small wounds.

He might not be human. But he was no god.

Very well; alone, then! he thought, and turned to the weary business of mankilling.

And, very suddenly, it was over. The Elphod was there in all his wrath, moonsilver glittering on his golden armor. An aerial chariot drawn by a dozen Phlygûl had borne him to the scene of battle. He stood erect, thundering imprecations in a mighty voice. How could the withered ancient stand up in the crushing weight of all that gold? wondered Silvermane. The old man's vigor was unnatural—superhuman.

He came striding through the carnage like a walking idol. To every side the battle clamor ceased and silence fell. As he came near a strange, pungent odor came to Ganelon's nostrils. Ah, that explained it, thought the giant, almost pityingly. The First Holy Elphod was addicted to the moon lotus drug which lent the user for a brief time the strength and vigor of thirty men. Often had he smelled that heady, magnolialike sweetness when passing through the Avenue of the Apothecaries back home in Zermish.

He leaned wearily on the pommel of the dripping sword as the gigantic golden figure strode clanking up to him.

In his right gauntlet the Elphod clutched a curious weapon. A rod of shimmering crystal, it was, terminating in a coppery cup. And that cup held a blazing sphere of naked energy. It seethed with brilliant fire like a miniature sun, that globe. Whatever the peculiar weapon was, Ganelon knew he was defenseless against it.

But he lifted the Silver Sword anyway, and took his

stand over the body of the unconscious Xarda, ready to fight on to the very last.

Eyes glinting coldly through the eye-slits of his golden mask, the Elphod lifted the scepter of atomic fire he had stolen from the ruins of Vandalex and pointed it at Ganelon Silvermane.

28.

THE FIRST
AND LAST ELPHOD

Time slowed down and stopped. Or so it seemed to the young giant as he stood there, staring into that miniature sun-ball of ravening atomic flame. Beyond the cup-shaped mouth of the weird crystal weapon, the eyes of the Holy Elphod glared into his own, no less burningly.

And then, quite suddenly, the scene changed. There came upon them a strangeness. Vapor rings gathered about the glittering golden figure. At first they were a mere misty blur in the air, like the quivering of rising heat-waves. Then the coils of misty stuff thickened into being, took on substance and reality.

One tapering coil was looped about the gauntleted wrist of the man clothed in gold. It tightened; metal creaked; the Elphod bellowed in surprise and pain. The crystal flame wand fell from his hand to the ground and lay there, smoldering the turf.

All at once the golden mesh toga and heavy gorget crumpled inward. The Elphod howled as if in the grip of some invisible force; he shrieked like a man with his hand in a vise. The gorget crumpled like a sheet of foil in a man's fist; bright blood jetted through the cracks and wrinkles in the gold. Then it was the golden helm and mask, crested with a tall miter. The helmet crushed in upon itself. The shrieking died to a choked gurgle, and ceased. Blood spurted from the eye-holes and the mouth-slit. The gold-clad body sagged lifelessly now, crushed and twisted, and hanging unsupported in the air.

Or *was* it unsupported? Ganelon strained his eyes through the moonlight, searching. Those coils of glassy transparency . . . and that blunt-nosed head lifting above the crushed, dangling figure . . . those dimly luminous eyes, like moon-pale opals . . . that lucent skull, crested with glistening plumes like sculptured ice. . . .

"Is it you, then, Jebd?" he inquired hoarsely.

The Sky Serpent nodded its floating head, great moon eyes aglow with friendly intelligence.

"Yessss, boy . . . Jebd," the Sky Serpent hissed.

"But where did you—? Why did—?" Ganelon fumbled for the proper question, but his wits were whirling and his brain felt numb with fatigue and marvel.

From behind the dangling golden corpse stepped the red lobsterlike figure of Fryx. The Gyraphont still held the tip of the Sky Serpent's tail gently between his nippers. Sudden relief and realization welled up within Ganelon; he sobbed with reaction. Of course! Fryx would never run away and leave them to perish; the Gyraphont had merely gone back to Nerelon and returned with reinforcements. And, of all the creatures housed by the Illusionist in his palace of enchantments, the most powerful and dangerous was the monster aerial python, Jebd.

You hokay? How Master? Where girl? What wrong with birdcritter? the Gyraphont chattered anxiously.

"And what do I do with—thisss?" asked the Sky Serpent, giving the dead thing in crumpled gold a shake in its powerful, transparent coils. The broken arms and legs flopped like those of a rag doll shaken in the hands of a playful child.

"You can drop him now, dear Jebd. Well done, my faithful Fryx!" said a quiet, familiar voice from behind Silvermane.

He turned; the Illusionist looked tired, and his silken robes were smudged with oil and dirtied by smears of graphite, and sparks that singed one sleeve to ebon tatters. But the blue shaft that rose above them hummed no more, and the brassy ball was dull and lusterless. The Death Machine itself was dead, never to be rekindled again.

The Illusionist lifted his head and looked beyond them to where the Sky Island soldiers stood in silent clumps about the trampled field. Their eyes were bewildered and frightened and dulled. The fires had gone out of them and they slumped tiredly, and many of them had let their weapons fall from their hands.

"You can all go home now," the Illusionist said to them quietly. "Take up your wounded and go home. You have lost the battle, you see; and it was your last battle." He laughed a little. "I imagine it was your first battle, too."

Then he pointed a gloved hand at the dead man in gold.

"Take that with you when you go. Your First Elphod; your First and Last Elphod, he is now. Go to your homes in peace, and come against us no more, or we shall destroy you to the last man and bring your city down in crashing ruin."

Slowly, the soldiers turned, dispersed, wandering away, silent and weary and dispirited. The Illusionist watched for a little as three of them, with considerable effort, began to drag the crushed golden thing toward its waiting chariot. Then he turned back to his friends again.

"Ganelon, sit down and rest; you are tired and I must look to your wounds. First, you will find a skin of wine in the tail compartment of the Bazonga. Drink your fill and get us all something to eat."

"But Xarda, master!"

"She is not slain; the electric weapons deal out a stunning shock that causes unconsciousness. Let me examine her; get the wine, and a skin of water, too."

Ganelon put his great sword down and stumbled wearily to the dead, floating machine and began to rummage through their baggage.

"What about the bird, master? Is it dead?"

The Illusionist shook his head.

"Her energy crystals are almost drained. She was never built for fighting, poor thing, and she exhausted her power source in helping you. But there are engines within the tower which still contain potent batteries I did not smash; it will be no great feat to reenergize the Bazonga. Now for the love of the Green Nexus, where's that cursed wine? I am dry as the Voormish Desert!"

They ate and drank and rested, speaking very little, while the stars wheeled overhead and the great, cracked, swollen bulk of the Falling Moon slowly traversed the dome of the heavens from edge to edge of the world.

Xarda recovered from her swoon weak and shaken and with a small burn on her forehead; but she had taken no serious hurt from the battle and soon recovered her vigor and cheerfulness. It did not prove difficult for the magician to patch together copper electrodes which he attached to the battery terminals, draining their stores of power to reenergize the dormant Bazonga. In no time the quaint vehicle was working again.

The Illusionist dispatched Jebd the Sky Serpent together with Fryx into the city to turn loose and drive away all of the Phlygûl who were housed in the roosting tower. The dawn-pink skies were made nightmarish for a time, as clouds of black-winged bat-monsters swarmed in the heavens above the metropolis of the former Airmasters; gradually the flying creatures dispersed to every point of the compass and the Illusionist laid a powerful enchantment upon the whole of Sky Island, which would ensure that never again while the world lasted would the Phlygûl nest on Sky Island.

"But what good does that do?" murmured Xarda.

"My dear child, with the Phlygûl driven away, never to return, the Sky Islanders are helplessly marooned here and cannot descend to bother the people of Karjixia or any other land. And I have rendered the Death Machine thoroughly useless. With the Elphod dead, there is no one else on Sky Island with sufficient scientific and technical training to repair it or use it to threaten the world with the mobile Death Zone again. For only that old maniac, Vlydabec, had studied the lost knowledge of Vandalex."

"So?" the girl snapped tartly.

"So, unless the once-high-and-mighty Airmasters want to starve themselves to death, they had better get busy farming the jungles for food. Because all commerce between them and the world below has been permanently terminated. They are stuck here, unable to raid or threaten or intimidate anyone else. They will have to feed themselves by the sweat of their brow, or die out."

He looked about him at the dawn-lit jungle, the grassy plains beyond, and the freshwater lake in the distance.

"This shouldn't be a bad place to live, once they learn to fend for themselves, instead of living off the labor of others," he said. "I will keep an eye on them to see they do not suffer."

"So that's it, then? You are not going to punish them any further, or wreak a more dire vengeance for all the fear and pain and death and suffering they have caused the Tigermen, and would have caused the people of many other lands?"

He shook his head. "No, my dear. I have already punished them more dreadfully than you can possibly imagine. I took from them their convictions of superiority. I took from them their very god, and showed his feet of clay. It is a cruel punishment, Xarda; a bitter lesson. To hurt them further would be superfluous."

"What do we do now, master? Do we go home?" asked Silvermane. The magician had treated his injuries with a powerful healing salve, and the giant had eaten and rested. He felt fit once again, although still bone-weary.

"I think not," said the Illusionist. "I shall send Fryx and Jebd back home to Nerelon, of course, for we need them no longer. But I believe that you and I owe it to our little friend here to see her safely back to Jemmerdy, or wherever it is that she wishes to go. We owe her that much, at least, for her assistance in this adventure."

It was not long after this that the Bazonga bird rose from the grassy clearing with Xarda and the Illusionist and Ganelon Silvermane in the cockpit. The sun was well up now; the morning air was fresh and bright and keen. The sky was a glorious blue, decorated here and there with small, crisply curled white clouds. Below them lay the immeasurable vastness of Old Earth's last and greatest continent, Gondwane the Great, thronged with its innumerable cities and nations and empires, filled with unexplored mountains and rivers, valleys and deserts, plains and forests, jungles and lakes. There dwelt strange people and mysterious beings, curious beasts and monsters. Supernatural creatures never known to men lurked in many a chasm and crevice and cave; conquerors and warlords, sorceresses and wizards, plotted and schemed, dreaming their dreams and working their marvels. A worldwide land lay beneath their flying keel, a world they had as yet only begun to explore, a world that held yet many strange and perilous adventures for them.

The sentient vehicle circled Sky Island under the morning sun. Then it flew off and dwindled into the distance, bound for new and even more wonderful adventures.

APPENDIX

A GLOSSARY OF UNFAMILIAR NAMES AND TERMS

Appendix:

A GLOSSARY OF UNFAMILIAR
NAMES AND TERMS

Death Dwarfs:

A repulsive but hardy form of Antilife, sufficiently sentient to be easily corrupted into subservience for destructive purposes. The bald, diminutive, green-skinned bipeds are a grimly humorless and unlikable species, vicious by natural inclination, and extremely inimical to all other sentients. They subsist on a diet of liquid poisons, ground glass, and other inedible substances, as is usual for the reversed metabolism of their kind; normal or more wholesome varieties of nutriment are to them deadly and poisonous. They chiefly inhabit the so-called Mountains of the Death Dwarfs, preferring the bleak, sterile slopes and noisome craters and caverns to more amenable environments. At the time period in which this book is set several of the easternmost clans have come under the dominance of the Queen of Red Magic.

Galendil the Good:

The supreme divinity worshiped by the inhabitants of the Gondwane continent during this Eon and that following. According to the tenets of several related sects or creeds, Galendil was the lone survivor of previous pantheons formerly worshiped but since outmoded by the evolution of newer religions. His worship crops up in the most unlikely places; in the Zul-and-Rashemba mythos for example (*q.v.*).

Godmaking, art of:

An art-form unique to the inhabitants of Gondwane during this Eon and that immediately previous; as intimations of newly developed divinities appear in the inspired imaginations of their prophets, or are invented by them, Godmakers are commissioned to intuit their likenesses and attributes, which they subsequently execute in sculpture for the adoration of the new sects. Masters of this difficult art are excessively rare, as an unusual degree of sensitivity and emotional empathy, to say nothing of intuition itself, are required of the Godmaker if he is to presage with accuracy the lineaments and vocations of yet-unborn divinities. Phlesco of Zermish, incidentally, lived with his wife some forty-nine years beyond the period of his appearance in this book of the Epic to become one of the most renowned and celebrated Godmakers of his age; successive generations of his fellow artisans held his achievements in the highest degree of veneration.

Gyraphonts:

A species of tomb-dwelling, grave-robbing, soul-devouring lobster-ghouls, part of the common mythologies of several related Gondwanian creeds, notably the Vemenoid and the Sarzanian. Not entirely indigenous to this plane, nor composed of Real Matter (except in the occult or metaphysical definition of the term), they are peculiarly difficult to pursue, hunt, capture, imprison, or train, since their capabilities include the handy use of interdimensional shortcuts. They are usually depicted in religious art as erect and bulbous, clad in scarlet chitin, with twenty-seven limbs, mandibles, or pincers, and possessing from nine to thirteen distinct eyes. Since they are at once dangerous, elusive, and predatory, from his domestication of certain Gyraphonts, notably Fryx, the reader may deduce something of the extraordinary abilities of the Illusionist of Nerelon.

Horxite Faith:

Essentially an offshoot of Polydeuxianity, the Horxite faith (originally, the "Horxite heresy") includes several tenets borrowed or derived from Margonomy and Old High Panduxism among its dogmas. Established by Hor the Revelator in the 940th Millennium of the Eon, the religious system is structured upon the inspired teachings contained in the Ninety Scriptures, and celebrates a pantheon composed of Gulnazphaz and six lesser Gods; originally conceived as a septitheism by the Revelator, the doctrine was later defined by the twenty-third Hierophant as an attenuated monotheism, since the remaining six divinities of the septitheism are now considered but facets or avatars of the seventh, who is Gulnazphaz himself. (Galendil the Good figures in the Horxite mythos, as in many others; in Horxite terms, he is Nerelus the Shadowmaker.)

Illusionist of Nerelon:

This enigmatic and shadowy personage was, in his time, ranked as one of the supreme thaumaturgists in the Gondwane continent. The secret of his origin, identity, and true name have thus far successfully eluded the researches of innumerable generations of commentators and redactors of that great work, the *Exemplary Life and Heroic Exploits of Ganelon Silvermane*, from which enduring masterpiece the present book and its sequels are derived. The general consensus of scholars, however, is that whoever he actually was, he was probably a native of Northern YamaYamaLand, perhaps even a native of the Hegemonic city of Oryx, to which, it will be recalled, he flees for refuge at the approach of the Indigon horde (see Bk. I, Chap. 5). As Yllth, editor of the Eleventh Redaction of the *Exemplary Life*, was the first to point out, whatever his origins he was, very obviously, more than merely an Illusionist. (The term was generally employed, at royal court or in traveling carnivals, for an entertainer who concocted harmless and insubstantial pageants, tableaux, or spectacles for the amusement of an audience.) At various places he exhibits mastery of the arts of wizardry, necromancy, sorcery, warlockry, and pansprexy. The veiled features, the anonymity, and the extraordinary magical powers he displays on several occasions has led some scholars to consider him either an Avatar or a Sending.

Indigons:

Quasianthromorphs of considerable weight, strength, and ferocity, sufficiently intelligent to employ rude tools and weapons. They commonly herd on the Purple Plains north of Karjixia and Phynx, but their migratory instinct makes them formidable invaders of more civilized countries when, in certain seasons, they stampede. It is believed that the Indigons were bred in the vats of Uxorian Maximus, a prominent magician of the Eon.

Phloigms:

The three organs of supernatural preception located in the cortex of the human forebrain between the cerestium gland and the outermost ovules of the peripexian system. The first of the three, the *celestial*, is the phloigm by which visitations, inspirations, or prophetic visions of the Gods may be observed; the second, or *demonic*, phloigm serves the same usages as regards evil spirits of the infernal plane; the third, or *elemental*, enables one to perceive nature spirits, genii and the like. Now largely vestigial, save in certain rare individuals, fully developed phloigmal systems were the rule rather than the exception in previous Eons.

Vandalex:

The name of an immensely powerful Technological Empire which flourished nearly ten million years before the lifetime of Ganelon Silvermane. It was located in northwestern Gondwane, beyond the Plains of Vlad, and was the dominant civilization of the Eon of the Flying Cities. The capital, Grand Phesion, still existed in Ganelon's time, and many of the robot mechanisms were actually functional. The Empire fell in war against the High Advocates of Tring, but was not completely extinguished in the intervening ages. Silvermane himself visited the ruins of Grand Phesion at the end of the Eon, according to the eighth book of the Epic. Not all of the scientific learning and wisdom of the Technarchs of Vandalex had vanished by Silvermane's time; libraries and documents still existed, and more than one of the amazing "cortexiums" (libraries of knowledge stored in a giant robot memory facility) were still operational; the Elphod of Sky Island, for instance, may have learned from a cortexium the technological data he later used to render the Death Zone of Karjixia mobile.

Yxium:

Element 127 on the Periodic Table; the known isotope of yxium possessing the longest half-life has an atomic weight of 280. The element is exceedingly rare, existing only in the cores of certain stars, particularly the so-called "neutron stars." In the form of a durable crystalline isotope with a half-life of several thousand years, it has been synthetically created on Earth by the use of fire magic. The molecular polarities of yxium are reversed, and the lattice structure of its particles are bent awry at a right angle to that of all other known elements; this is believed to be the factor which causes yxium crystals to reverse the gravitational field and hence "fall upward" instead of down.

Zul-and-Rashemba Mythos:

A Gondwanian religious system which interprets the entirety of universal history in the symbolism of domestic spats and periods of affectionate tranquility between the Goddess Zul (the Cosmic Overself) and her often-erring husband, the God Rashemba (the Universal Soul-Ocean). According to the tenets of this sect, the Divine Couple ruled the Earth for thirty-two thousand millennia before going on a second honeymoon to an adjoining space/time plenum.

They left the Earth, it is believed, in the care of their teen-aged son, Galendil, who was also instructed to watch over their former home atop Marmoramax the Cosmic Mountain (believed to exist at the exact center of the Gondwane supercontinent, and to achieve a height of 394 miles about the Earth). Galendil, however, prefers to reside elsewhere, it is said, being unfond of heights. The Time Gods also play an obscure part in this mythology, but their exact relationship to the Divine Family is difficult to ascertain due to ambiguities in the Scripture. The Phoenix-like Bazonga bird (the Messenger of Heaven) was a domestic pet of the Couple, and other mythological creatures figure in one or another manner in the mythos. Rashemba, by the way, was amusingly presented as an ordinary husband, employed to keep the Sun energized; and Zul, the typical housewife, had, among her numerous domestic duties, the task of polishing the Moon and replacing the stars when they burned out. The entire mythos is considered by some a degenerate popularization of Old High Great Quaxianity.